The Far Side of the Loch

The Far Side
of the Loch

Melissa Wiley

Illustrations by Renée Graef

HarperCollins*Publishers*

For my father and mother, Murray and Diane Brannon

*Special thanks to my brilliant researcher Caroline
Carr-Locke, to Professor Williamson of The School of Scottish
Studies, Edinburgh University, for his help with the language, and to
Janice Putnam, Damon Cook, Rich Pavlick, and Craig Borger of
Old Sturbridge Village in Sturbridge, Massachusetts, for providing me
with firsthand experience at sheep-shearing.*

HarperCollins®, 🌲®, Little House®, and The Martha Years™
are trademarks of HarperCollins Publishers Inc.

The Far Side of the Loch
Text copyright © 2000 by HarperCollins Publishers Inc.
Illustrations copyright © 2000 by Renée Graef
Printed in the United States of America. For information address
HarperCollins Children's Books, a division of HarperCollins Publishers,
1350 Avenue of the Americas, New York, NY 10019.
www.littlehousebooks.com

Library of Congress Cataloging-in-Publication Data
Wiley, Melissa.
   Far side of the Loch / Melissa Wiley ; illustrations by Renée Graef. —
1st HarperTrophy ed.
      p.   cm. — (The Martha years)
   Summary: Continues the childhood adventures in the Scottish coun-
tryside of seven-year-old Martha Morse who would grow up to become
the great-grandmother of author Laura Ingalls Wilder.
   ISBN 0-06-027984-2 — ISBN 0-06-028203-7 (lib. bdg.)
   [1. Family Life—Scotland—Fiction. 2. Scotland—Fiction.] I. Graef,
Renée, ill. II. Title.
PZ7.W64814 Far 2000   99-052653
[Fic]—dc21

                    1   2   3   4   5   6   7   8   9   10
                                    ❖
                          First Edition, 2000

Contents

On the Glass Mountain

The Stone House, which had been so crowded and jostling earlier in the winter, seemed all empty corners now. All day Martha's mother and sister worked quietly at their spinning, their knitting, their sewing. Mum was not herself; she was waiting tensely for Father's next letter.

Nearly three months had passed since Father had left the valley of Glencaraid in the company of Uncle Harry and his big family. Uncle Harry and Aunt Grisell and the cousins had come to the Stone House in late December for a long visit, and while they were there, the house had been as crowded as a sheep-yard in spring. There had been hardly a single corner of the house that someone was not using to sleep or read or sew or eat in. Cook had complained that it was like living in a thunderstorm, but Martha loved every noisy, bustling minute of it. Then Father and Uncle and Aunt and all the cousins had packed up and said good-bye, and without them it did seem as though a great storm had swept through the Stone House and left everything flattened and changed in its wake.

Terribly changed—for Father had taken Martha's two oldest brothers with him. It was time, he said, for Alisdair and Robbie to get some schooling of a higher quality than that offered by the little village school in Clachan across the lake. So Father enrolled them in a boarding school in faraway Edinburgh, where their cousins David and Harold were pupils. Mum said they would not come home until the summer holidays, and then only for a few weeks.

On the Glass Mountain

Martha could hardly believe it was true. Alisdair gone—Alisdair with his kind, absent-minded smile and his store of interesting things to talk about—there was not another soul in the valley who knew as much about steam engines and spinning mills and the revolutions of America and France as Alisdair did. Martha ached with missing him, and with missing Robbie, too. Robbie stirred things up; he made sparks fly. The Stone House was dull and sleepy without him.

At least Duncan, the youngest brother, had not been sent to Edinburgh yet. He was not yet nine; Father said another year at home would do him no harm. Even so, Duncan hardly ever *was* home. He still had to go to the village school across the lake. He left the Stone House before dawn and did not come home until suppertime.

Sometimes during the long, quiet winter days, Martha had said to herself that Duncan might as well be in Edinburgh, she saw so little of him. But in the evenings when he came in, puffing and half frozen from his walk around the lake, she took the thought back. It was better to see him for little bits of the day than not to see him at all.

When Duncan came home, the Stone House woke back up a little. He was always full of stories about the things that had happened in school that day: the dog that had trotted right into the schoolhouse and sat down at the dominie's feet, or the spark that had burned a hole through Ian Cameron's breeches while he was warming himself at the fire, or who had won at the ice-skating race during the dinner recess. Martha listened eagerly. She wished that time of day would never end, the little busy window between supper and bed. The rest of the day was too still.

After Father had reached Edinburgh, he had written to say that he planned to stay on in the city for a while.

I must have taken leave of my senses, he wrote in a letter that Mum read aloud after supper one evening, *to allow Harry to persuade me that such a journey was possible at this frigid time of year. I shall stay where I am until the weather breaks—I've had enough of battling the icy roads of winter and would rather try my chances against spring and mud.*

Now the ice was melting, and the chill rains and mists of April were scrubbing winter away. The skating races melted out of Duncan's stories, replaced by tales of footraces and rock-throwing games.

One afternoon it actually stopped raining for a while, and the housemaid, Mollie, threw open the window shutters to air out the house. Martha had been sitting by the fire in Mum's room, nibbling on a bannock left over from the noon meal. Popping the last morsel of the oatbread into her mouth, she ran to look out the window and breathe in the cool air.

The fresh wind blew into the room and made the fire leap in the hearth. Bits of ash fluttered out into the room, and Martha's sister, Grisie, snatched up her sewing in a panic that a spark would singe her work.

"Canna we leave the shutters closed, Mother?" Grisie pleaded, and Mum nodded regretfully.

"I suppose we'd better, until the wind settles. Pull your head in, Martha, before you lose your balance and fall."

"I only wanted to see if the spring had come yet," Martha said.

It was not quite here, not yet. But Martha could smell its nearness in the wet air. Mollie closed the shutters, but it was too late; the fresh wind had gotten inside Martha and made her want to run and shout. She did not talk more loudly or clatter her feet on the floorboards on purpose, but it was true that Mum kept having to shush her, to remind her to behave like a young lady.

"Go and play with your fairy dolls, Martha," Mum said at last.

But even the fairy dolls were too noisy, it seemed. Martha tried to explain that it was *necessary* for the fairy baby to shriek at the top of its lungs for its mother, for how else could the mother remember where she had left it? Grisie rolled her eyes and asked the air why on earth it was that Martha's dolls could not be nice and quiet like other girls' dolls.

"Why do you no give the bairn a lullaby?"
Mum suggested; but singing lullabies made
Martha feel sleepy herself. On days like this
the whole house felt like one enormous box
bed, closed and shuttered and quiet.

At last Mum sent her outside. "You're really
too big a lass to run wild in the hills," she
said, sighing. "Past seven years old as you are!
But I'm sure I dinna ken what else to do with
you. It cuts my heart to see you pacing up
and down the room like a caged beast. Go out
and play yourself, my dear—only mind you
wrap up well against the wet."

So Martha raced out of the Stone House
with her long red curls streaming out beneath
the edges of Mum's old tartan shawl. At first
she thought she would go around behind the
house and climb the garden wall, and then she
thought she'd rather go down to the barns or
the farmers' cottages, to see if anything interesting was happening there.

But in the end she went to the Creag.

The Creag was a hill that rose in a steep,
rocky mass from the edge of Loch Caraid. It

was Martha's own special place, and she had missed going there all winter. She could not remember the last time she had gone—it would have been before the cousins arrived. Whenever it was, she hadn't known it would be the last time she'd climb the hill for months and months. As she ran toward the Creag, hurrying past the cottages and scrambling along the lakeshore, she had a strange feeling of going to visit an old friend who might possibly be angry with her for having stayed away so long. She would have said good-bye for the winter, if she'd known last time was indeed the last.

The Creag had once been the favorite haunt of all the Morse children, before Grisie grew too big for unladylike games and the boys began to live their lives at school. The eastern face of the hill, all grass and gorse bushes, sloped gently down to a stretch of vast, treeless, grassy moor. Its western face was the steep and rocky one, looking out upon Loch Caraid. From its shoulders Martha could see clear across the valley—the wide lake spread

out beneath the misty green mountains opposite, the cottages where Father's tenants lived,
the flax field, and the peat hags where the
tenants cut slabs of peat grass to burn in all
the fireplaces of the valley.

Martha came to the foot of the Creag and
looked upward. There was a story Mum told
about a lass who had to climb a glass mountain to rescue a giant bull, the fierce Black
Bull of Norroway. Martha thought she would
play that the Creag was the glass mountain,
and a mob of trolls was waiting at the top to
fight her for the bull, who was really a prince
under a cruel enchantment. It was great fun
to imagine she was climbing a hill so steep
and smooth that she kept sliding down it.

It would have been more fun if the hill had
really been made of glass. But Martha was so
glad to be out of the house that she did not
in the least mind pretending.

She was climbing the slick glass, and slipping down again, and painstakingly climbing
back up all the way to the top where the trolls
were lurking, when something caught her

eye—distant shapes moving on one of the green mountains that flanked Loch Caraid.

She stood up and stared across the lake. When she narrowed her eyes and looked very hard, she could make out a horse and rider making their way along the steep path. Behind them came something else, two somethings, moving together at a slow, jolting pace.

Martha knew at once that the rider was Father and behind him was a boy leading a pony. Her heart leaped.

Father had come home at last!

Now perhaps the house would come awake again. Martha scrambled to the top of the Creag, where the view was best. She had quite forgotten the glass mountain and the terrible trolls. The Black Bull of Norroway would not break free of his enchantment today. Martha was watching Father's horse and the boy and pony behind him. There was a kind of magic in the slow, awkward movement of the dark shapes between the mountain and the lake.

Father looked terribly small. It seemed to Martha she could put out a hand and snatch him up, horse and all, if she wanted to.

She watched just a moment more, and then she was off, running like a hare to tell the others. She flew along the lakeshore and back past the cluster of tenant cottages. At the last cottage she stuck her head in the open doorway and cried, "Mrs. Sandy! Father's home, and Neil!"

A trio of startled faces looked up at Martha: Mrs. Sandy's youngest children, playing jackstraws on the rough earth floor of the cottage. Mrs. Sandy turned halfway around from the pot she was hanging over the peat fire.

"Mercy!" she declared, and then: "Och, Miss Martha, is it? Sure and ye gave me a fright. What's that ye say? His lairdship's come home?"

"And Neil," Martha repeated, gasping from her run. Mrs. Sandy was the wife of Father's steward, and her boy Neil had gone to the city with Father to look after his horse. "I saw them on the mountain. I must tell Mum—" and before Mrs. Sandy could say anything, Martha dashed back outside and raced up the hill toward the Stone House. Faintly behind her she heard the glad sounds of Neil's little brothers and sister, cheering because their brother had come home.

By the time Father's horse came around the bend of the lake, Martha and Mum and Grisie were outside waiting for him, with best dresses hurriedly put on so that they might look their finest for Father. Mum's cheeks were pink, and her blue eyes shone. She wore a silk gown of dark blue, the color of the sky the moment after the sun has set, with a black velvet ribbon tied around the high waist. Her rich brown hair flowed in shining waves away from her brow to a waterfall of curls high above her neck.

Grisie was as tall as Mum now—taller, if she dressed her hair high. But Father always said he liked to see a lass look like a lass. When Martha had run in shouting that Father was home, Grisie had quickly unpinned the dark locks piled high on her head and smoothed them into a knot at the nape of her neck. She had the kind of hair that stayed coiled smooth and neat even when the wind gusted, as it gusted now.

Martha's own curls blew into her face; she tossed them back with a shake of her head. Mum said the ribbon hadn't been invented yet that could bind Martha's thick hair. Mum had made her change into a clean frock, her new red plaid, and for once Mum had said Martha need not cover up her dress with a muslin dust-gown. It felt almost like Sunday to Martha—a new frock and no dust-gown, and Mum wearing silk!

Father's steward, Sandy, stood by the loupin'-on stone, a large round boulder in the middle of the yard, ready to take Father's horse. Sandy's lined face beamed proudly to see his son Neil grown so tall and fine-looking during the months in the faraway city. Through the open kitchen window came the sound of a spoon clattering in a pot, and Cook's voice, at once pleased and grumbling, calling out instructions to Nannie, the plump, yellow-haired kitchenmaid. Cook was hurrying to make a homecoming supper. Martha had eaten a big dinner that noon, but she felt hungry again, smelling the tantalizing kitchen smells.

Father's horse pranced up the hill as if it were fresh out of the stable and not wearied with days of hard travel. It tossed its head and shook its windblown mane and hurried the last few paces toward the yard: It knew it was home at last. Neil came jogging behind it, holding the pony's reins in one hand and waving his cap in the other. His sunburned face was all smiling eyes and mouth.

Father, atop the great brown horse, took his hat off too, his big rounded bonnet, and waved it in greeting.

"Father! Father!" Martha shouted, jumping up and down.

Father was tall as a giant upon the great horse, nothing like the tiny figure Martha had seen on the hill. The horse came thundering toward the house and for half a second Martha thought, *It's not going to stop*—but it did. Father leaped off its back onto the loupin'-on stone. Martha could see he was as glad to be home as Martha and Mum and Grisie were to see him. He strode forward, took Mum's hand, kissed it in a polite, citified way; then, chuckling, he pulled her into his arms and squeezed her.

"Good day, Missus Morse," he said, laughing. Mum smiled up at him and said, "Good day, Mr. Morse."

Father kissed Grisie and swept Martha into his arms, saying how fine it was to be home. Of all the places he had seen on the way to Edinburgh and back, he said, not a one could hold a candle to his own Glencaraid.

He said he had thought to be home before the midday meal, but at the last minute he had decided to stop at Fairlie. Fairlie was the house Father had grown up in; it stood in a glen a mile or so away from the opposite shore of Loch Caraid, overlooking the South Loch farm.

Father's estate was divided into four farms— Glencaraid, which was named after the whole valley; South Loch; and two smaller spreads, Glenmorris and Pennidrue, that Father leased to tenant farmers. A cousin of Father's had leased the big house at South Loch some years

past, but he was gone now, to India. The South Loch farmers came across the lake to Glencaraid several times a year to pay their rents directly to Father. Fairlie was empty except for an aging steward, Albert, and his grown-up daughter Alice, who served as housekeeper.

"Auld Albert must be nigh eighty by now," Mum murmured, and Father nodded.

"Aye, he's past doing any kind of work. Happen I ought to have brought him over here when we built this house. But he'd lived and worked at Fairlie so long, it would have been hard on him to be uprooted."

Father stretched, shaking out the stiffness of the long hours he had spent on horseback.

"Well, Albert's in grand hands with Alice," he went on. "The salt o' the earth, she is, and a grand manager. I fear her talents are wasted on that empty house. She ought to have a passel o' servants to order about; she'd keep 'em in sharp order, all right! I tell you, Margaret, seeing the auld place put a thought in my head—but I shall no tell you what it is until it's grown up a bit."

"Nay, Father, tell it now!" Martha cried eagerly.

But Father looked at her with arched eyebrows and said, "I said I shall wait, and wait I shall."

So Martha did not find out his secret that day.

But there were other secrets to discover—all sorts of bags and parcels bundled on the pony's back. Sandy and Neil untied them and carried everything into the house. Father brushed the dust of traveling off his clothes and followed Mum and Grisie into the house. Martha hurried in after them, eager to know what treasures Father might have brought home from the capital city.

"To a Mouse"

Inside the Stone House it felt like a holiday. Everyone crowded into the hall while Sandy and Neil sorted the parcels into two piles: things that belonged in the kitchen and larder, and things that didn't. Cook and Nannie hurried out of the kitchen to greet Father and say how glad they were to have him home. Cook's broad face was red and shining. A savory aroma of roasting meat wafted out of the kitchen behind her.

Father sniffed appreciatively and said with

19

some surprise, "That's not rabbit I smell, Cook?"

"Aye," said Cook, "that it is. Do ye think, sir, I'd welcome ye home with no mair than a bannock and a curtsey? Said to Nannie, I did, 'There be no tellin' what kind o' horrible tavern fare the master has had to choke down on the way home, and I'll not sleep tonight if I dinna give him the first good halesome meal he's had in who kens how long.'"

Martha tried to guess what was inside each bag and bundle. Some were easy—a heavy sack that felt gritty when she squeezed it was sure to have sugar inside; another sack with a fragrant, leafy, musty scent was bound to be tea. But there were packages all tied up with brown paper and string whose contents Martha could not begin to guess. Her fingers tugged experimentally at a loose end of string.

"Martha!" Mum called, making Martha jump. "Leave that be, and get out from under Sandy's feet. Into the parlor with you, lass."

In the parlor Mollie had already poured a mug of ale for Father. She stood smiling by the sideboard, looking very pink and scrubbed in her starched white apron and snowy linen cap.

Father took the mug and raised it, as if he were toasting the room. His jacket and plaid kilt were faded and travel stained, and his knee stockings were splattered with mud from the road. His red hair was pulled back simply into a tail behind his neck, the way Martha liked it best. When he dressed for company he wore a wig, powdered and curled, as all gentlemen did; but the finest wig in the world would not hold up to a long journey on the bumpy tracks that passed for Highland roads. Even without the wig he looked grand and imposing. He was very tall. Looking at him, Martha felt a little awed: He had been gone for such a long time.

After he had taken a long sip of the ale, he sighed and said, "Ah, that's fine. Naught slakes the thirst like the home brew."

Then he went to the hall, picked out a few of the parcels from the pile at the foot of the stairs, and carried them into the parlor.

He had brought home presents for everyone. For Grisie there were yards and yards of a beautiful printed cotton cloth. It was a creamy white with red roses unfolding upon it, like an enchanted garden blooming in the snow.

"Your aunt Grisell helped me choose it," Father told Grisie. "They've a marvelous selection of fabrics in the shops in town. I'd have been quite helpless to pick among them, had your aunt no come along. A shrewd bargainer, she is—but then, with four lasses to clothe, I suppose she'd better be."

The cotton was soft against the skin, and it draped in beautiful flowing folds when Grisie held it against her like a skirt. Father said Edinburgh was fair drowned in cotton, and Glasgow even more so. It came by the shiploads from America, and every time you turned around, a new cotton mill had sprung up somewhere in Scotland.

He showed Martha a large, flat parcel and told her it was a kite for Duncan. Her heart leaped, for she had always wanted a kite herself. But the package he gave her was too small to be one. It was a flat, hard parcel wrapped in brown paper and tied with string.

Father cut the strings with his knife; inside the paper was a book—no, two books! Martha was astonished. Two books, for her very own. This was not the same kind of wonderful as a kite, but it was wonderful nonetheless.

One of the books was called *Six Prints of the Famous Dick Whittington and His Cat.* Martha knew that story; Mum had told it to her. And here it was now *in pictures*, with the handsome talking cat looking just as she had imagined he would.

The second book was called *Hook's Easy Lessons*, and the pages inside were filled with music for the pianoforte. Father said he hoped this book would improve Martha's playing a great deal. Privately, Martha doubted it would—she did not have Grisie's talent for music (though Mum said the only thing Martha lacked was Grisie's talent for practicing). But she thanked Father politely for the

Hook's, and for the *Dick Whittington* she gave him a loud, smacking kiss on the cheek.

Now it was Mum's turn. The brown parcel Father placed upon her lap was chunky and solid; Mum looked it over and said she could not guess what it might be. Eagerly she opened it, with everyone watching. Then she could not speak—none of them could.

It was a box of polished wood, in the shape of a pianoforte. It sat upon four slender carved legs, and the keyboard was carved with tiny keys. It was beautiful, and Mum's breath caught as she looked at it.

But there was more to it than beauty. Father showed Mum how the top of the piano lifted up on tiny hinges. Inside were a dozen small compartments of varying sizes. There was a pair of silver scissors in one compartment, and a needle case in another, and some spools of silk thread in a third. The rest were empty, for Mum to fill with her own sewing things.

"Allan, you shouldna have," Mum said, and her eyes were shining.

"Look at the darling wee keys carved on it," said Grisie.

Father nodded. "Aye, that's fine craftsmanship. You'll not see finer."

"If the keys worked," said Martha, "they'd be just the right size for a fairy to play."

"Ah, but it would be fairy music," Mum said, "and you ken how dangerous that is to hear. The tunes would catch us in our dreams and keep us stuck there dreaming until the house crumbled to dust around us."

Grisie shuddered. She didn't like to think about such things.

Martha reached out to touch the tiny perfect keys. She wondered if Tullie Grayshanks, the brownie who lived in the Stone House, would find the pianoforte that night and be disappointed that it was not a real one for him to play.

It hardly seemed possible that Father could have brought home anything more wonderful than the pianoforte box. But last of all he brought out another book, a small one with a brown leather spine and a marbled cover.

On the brown spine was a red square that was inscribed with the words:

BURNS
POEMS

The poems inside had been written, Father said, by a farmer from Ayrshire in the Lowlands. He had become the talk of Edinburgh. Some people there spoke of him as a Scottish treasure.

"Do you remember the verses I read to you from *Edinburgh Magazine* some months back?" Father asked Mum. "The poem about the daisy that you liked so much?"

"Aye, I mind it well," Mum said, her face lighting up. "I thought it was lovely. These are by that same—what was his name—Robert Burns? Allan, how marvelous! Come, let's hear something now."

Father emptied his mug of ale. Standing tall and straight before the window, where the light was best, he said, "Here's one I like quite well—called 'To a Mouse,' it is, 'On Turning Her up in her Nest with the Plough':

"To a Mouse"

"Wee, sleekit, cowrin', tim'rous beastie,
O, what a panic's in thy breastie!
Thou need na start awa sae hasty,
Wi' bickering brattle!
I wad be laith to rin an' chase thee,
Wi' murd'ring pattle!"

Martha listened, spellbound, as Father continued to read. The words were like music, a beautiful, spinning, heartbreaking song. She felt so sorry for the poor mouse, whose nest had been ruined by Mr. Burns's plow. She could just see it there, the tiny sleek creature cowering in fear amid its broken nest of leaves and the hay stubble, with the turned-up earth all around it. Mr. Burns's words made the picture very vivid in her mind. She saw exactly how the mouse would dart hastily away, with its little heart thumping in terror. If only the mouse could understand the farmer's words, and know that he would not take up his paddle and chase after her!

Father read on:

"Thou saw the fields laid bare an' waste,
An' weary winter comin' fast
An' cozie here, beneath the blast,
Thou thought to dwell—

And then the farmer's plow had cut through and torn apart the cozy nest, just when the mouse was planning to spend the winter there. It seemed a very sad poem. But Martha thought she liked Mr. Burns, because he felt just as sorry for the mouse as she did. He hadn't *meant* to plow up the nest.

Martha didn't understand all of it, but she liked it. Grisie was listening with bright eyes and clasped hands. Father had told them how the whole city of Edinburgh was wild for Mr. Robert Burns, how his poems were read aloud at every gathering.

He was just beginning the final stanza when Duncan burst into the parlor, making them all jump. There was suddenly a busy sound of footsteps in the hallway behind him, and Cook's voice was very loud, calling out orders to Nannie. Martha and the others had been so caught up in the verses that no one had realized how late it was getting.

"Nearly suppertime, it is," Mum exclaimed, "and you still in your traveling clothes, Allan! That rabbit must be just about ready for the table now."

Duncan was grinning all over his face, he was so glad to have Father home. Father clapped him on the back, said he was looking well, and made him conjugate a few Latin verbs to see if he had kept at his lessons. He gave Duncan the marvelous kite, a shimmering thing of red and green silk.

"Let's go and try it now!" Martha cried, and Mum laughed and said they'd do no such thing, what with supper coming to the table at any minute. So they all went upstairs instead, to wash up before the meal.

When they had gathered again at the table in Mum and Father's bedroom, Mum asked Father to finishing reading "To a Mouse."

"Och, aye, Father," begged Grisie. "Please do!"

"I'll start it over," said Father, "so Duncan can hear."

While he was reading, Mollie came into the room carrying a platter of boiled beef and cheese. Slowly she placed the dishes on the table, not at all with her usual brisk movements. When the tray was empty, she lingered in the doorway, listening, and then reluctantly turned to go back to the kitchen for the roast.

But it was not Mollie who appeared a moment later, bearing a dish of roasted rabbit dripping with onion gravy—it was Cook, red-faced and puffing. Martha was so surprised to see her that she almost fell out of her chair. She cried out, interrupting Father.

"Save us and bless us!"

There was a moment's startled silence. Father stared at Martha with arched eyebrows over the red book. He looked at Cook and back at Martha again.

"Beg pardon, Father," Martha gasped. "But—Cook!"

She could not remember ever having seen Cook in Mum's room before. Cook *never* came upstairs. She worked in the kitchen and she slept in the kitchen, and when she wanted to "sit a spell and rest," she sat and rested in the kitchen. Seeing her standing between Father's writing desk and the dinner table was like seeing the minister in a sheep barn, or Mum perched on top of a haystack.

Cook raised her shoulders indignantly. "Can I no lend a hand to poor Mollie without bringin' the world to an end?"

Mollie, who had come back into the room behind Cook, made a choking sound that was something between a snort and a laugh. She hid a smile behind her hand.

Father's eyes were twinkling. "Come, now, Cook, confess it—you wanted to hear how the poem ended, didna you?"

"I'd not presume to contradict ye, sir," Cook said, setting the roast on the table. Her voice was crushingly haughty.

Martha knew that meant Father was right— for Cook would not hesitate to contradict the King himself, if she believed he was wrong. Father chuckled, and Mollie was laughing out-right.

Mollie said, "We were all of us listenin', sir, when ye were readin' in the parlor. And then when Master Duncan came home and ye stopped, it fair drove us crazy wonderin' how the thing ended. When I told them downstairs ye was readin' it over again, Cook, she snatched up the roast and ran for the stairs. Och, I've no seen someone move so fast since the time Gavin Tervish's roof caught fire!"

Everyone was laughing now. Cook threw her hands in the air and said, "That tongue o' yours wants tyin' down, Mollie McDermott," but she was grinning too.

Father said they'd better have the whole thing over again, from start to finish, so everyone could hear. "Call for Nannie," he said. "We might as well have the whole house in from the start this time."

"I'm right here, sir," said Nannie, ducking into the room. She had been standing in the hall the whole time. This made Father roar with laughter again. Martha and Duncan howled; Mum was dabbing at her eyes with

32

a napkin. But Grisie was earnestly hushing everyone so that Father could read the poem.

" 'To a Mouse," he said at last, "On Turning Her up in her Nest . . .' "

Though she had heard it nearly three times through now, there was still much about the poem Martha did not understand. But she understood that there was a power to it, for where everyone had been laughing so hard a moment before, they were all hushed and serious now. Grisie's forehead had a little crease down the center, and her eyes were full of thought. Martha had forgotten how hungry she was; she had forgotten everything but the mouse.

"But Mousie, thou art no thy lane,
In proving foresight may be vain:
The best-laid schemes o' mice an' men
Gang aft agley,"

Father read.

You are not alone, little mouse—Martha liked the sound of it so much, and the thought that people and mice had something in common. Anyone, anyone, mouse or man, could have his plans turned upside down like the poor mouse's nest. Martha thought of last winter, when her beautiful doll, Lady Flora, had been lost in the icy waters of Loch Caraid. That had certainly not been part of Martha's plans. . . .

But when Father came to the last stanza, she did not understand at all.

> *"Still thou art blest, compared wi' me!*
> *The present only toucheth thee:*
> *But och! I backward cast my e'e,*
>   *On prospects drear!*
> *An' forward, tho' I canna see,*
>   *I guess an' fear!"*

Though all the grown-ups let out their held breath and nodded their heads, Martha felt surprised. Who could be afraid to look forward to the future, when tomorrow after tomorrow after tomorrow waited beckoning and bright with promise?

Sour Grisie

Father had so much to tell of his journey that he talked all the next day, and still he had not told it all. He told of the Academy where Robbie and Alisdair where now working hard at their studies. He told of the busy streets of Edinburgh, and fishwives going from house to house with their baskets of fish strapped to their backs, and of houses built so close together that their walls touched each other. Martha tried to picture it all, but it was hard to imagine. Father described the town house in which Uncle Harry's family lived:

They lived on the middle floor, with two families above them and two families below them.

Martha listened to all of it as eagerly as if she had not eaten in a week and Father was dishing out almond-cream and strawberries. Father never told stories. Mum did, wonderful stories; and Cook did, and Alisdair, and Sandy, and wise Auld Mary who lived on the moor—but not Father, laird of Glencaraid. Now he was telling them, and what was more, they were real and true, about people Martha knew and places she was suddenly on fire to visit someday. So much was happening in the wide world beyond her own valley.

Duncan was away at school all day and missed most of Father's stories. When he came home at suppertime, Martha begged Father to tell them all over again. Father gave a mock groan and said he'd trust the telling to Martha.

"Sure and you asked so many questions," he said, "that I'm thinking by now you must ken mair about Edinburgh than I do."

"Och, nay," Martha pleaded. "You tell it best, Father. Grisie and Mum willna mind hearing it again—will you?"

"Of course not." Mum laughed. So Father described it all for Duncan, all the sights of Edinburgh. Martha chimed in to help him remember the best parts—the fishwives, the strange houses, Alisdair and Robbie looking stiff and solemn in their new school clothes.

There was one thing Father would not tell, and that was his secret. Martha tried to coax it out of him, but he only raised his eyebrows in a way that meant she had better stop asking. He would tell it when he was ready.

But he did tell of Edinburgh Castle, and the University, and the tall-masted ships docked at the port in the Firth of Forth, the great bay that led to the sea. He told of the endless round of parties and dinners that Uncle Harry and Aunt Grisell went to, and the dances that kept Janet and Meg out until the wee hours of the night.

"And Meg a full year younger than Grisie. It's scandalous, in my opinion," he said sternly.

Grisie, Martha noticed, did not look as if she agreed.

After that, Martha and Duncan talked of nothing but Edinburgh. There was no end to new, absorbing games to play in the evenings after supper. Duncan took out his paints and began an ambitious picture of Edinburgh street life, full of carriages and wagons and staggeringly tall houses. Father watched the painting's progress with great interest, offering helpful bits of advice about such things as the size and shape of the paving-stones, the colors of house doors, and the kind of hats worn by carriage drivers and footmen.

"I must say, though, you've rather a lot o' cattle there in the street, lad," he said. "I dinna recall seeing mair cows than human beings, when I was there."

"Aye," Duncan said sheepishly, "but I'm a much better hand at painting cattle than people. It's the clothes—I dinna ken exactly what to paint. Cattle are easier."

Father nodded. "Ah, there is that. Well, why do you not get your sisters to pose for you? All the great painters use models. Let the lasses rig up some costumes to help you out."

Martha was bewitched by the notion. "Och, aye! I'll be a fishwife! May I, please, Mum?"

"A fishwife! Well, it's an honest living," Mum teased. "Aye, let's see what we can find."

She called in Mollie, and together they rummaged through chests and closets for a suitable costume. A faded old red napkin was deemed the perfect kerchief to cover Martha's head, and Mollie ran up to the attic for a stained and patched dress that she saved for hearth-cleaning days. Mum helped Martha into the dress, wrapped a worn gray shawl around her shoulders, and tied the red napkin around her head. She emptied some skeins of yarn out of a woven straw basket and strapped the basket to Martha's back.

"There! Hunch over a little, as if it's heavy," Mum instructed. "You'll have to make believe the fish are there—I'll not have you standing here filling up the room wi' the smell o' dried fish!"

Then she clapped her hands and said Martha couldn't look more like a fishwife if she'd been born one. Duncan was very pleased, and he immediately set to work painting Martha into his picture.

"Pull out a few strands o' hair about your face," he said. "Straggly like. Aye, that's it. Now look tired—and hungry. I want to get the expression just right."

Martha tried, but it was hard not to laugh. It was harder yet to stand still, and Duncan kept scolding her not to fidget. She closed her eyes and tried to really feel like an old fish-wife, trudging from door to door along the busy town street. But with Mum and Father laughing at her, and the gray shawl making her uncomfortably warm, and a lock of hair tickling her cheek, she could not feel like anyone but Martha Morse. Nevertheless it was great fun. She kept wanting to run around and look at Duncan's picture, and he kept ordering her to stay where she was.

"Your turn next, Grisie!" Martha cried. "You ought to put on Mum's blue silk, and pretend you're a fine young lady off to a ball!"

But Grisie did not want to play. She said

stiffly that she wanted to finish embroidering the collar she was working on. Martha stared at her curiously, but Grisie did not look up from her sewing. Her fingers were stabbing the needle into the cloth.

Duncan shrugged and said he doubted he'd finish the fishwife that night anyway.

"That's right," Mum said brightly. "A painting of this scope will likely take days to finish. Grisie can model for you another night."

That was the first time Martha noticed that something was wrong with Grisie. After that she noticed it all the time.

Grisie was very cross. Every morning she complained that she hadn't a single gown fit to wear; and when Father was out of the house, she spent long hours experimenting with new ways of dressing her hair. She scolded Martha for calling Mum and Father's bedroom "Mum and Father's bedroom"—as if that was not what everyone in the house had called it for as long as Martha could remember!

"It ought properly to be called 'the spence,'" Grisie corrected her. "Janet and Meg said so when they were here."

On the spot Martha made a secret vow never, ever to say "the spence"—not if Grisie had taken the idea from Cousin Janet and Cousin Meg. She was tired of hearing about Janet and Meg, who were evidently such wonderful company that Grisie had liked sleeping with them in a cold, drafty corner of the attic better than snuggling into her own warm nursery bed with Martha. Ever since the cousins had left last winter and Grisie had moved back into the nursery, she had grumbled about needing a room of her own.

Martha had had her own set of cousins to share a bed with during the holidays—Rachel, who was seven like Martha, and little five-year-old Mary. The truth was, Martha had found it rather interesting to be the one in charge of the bed for a while. Rachel and Mary were not used to box beds; their bed at home was one of the new open beds with tall posts at the corners. They had been scared inside the dark box with its wooden walls and low ceiling, and they clung to Martha and said she must be very brave to have slept in a black cave all her life. Martha had had a grand time thinking up stories to tell them, to take their minds off their fear of the dark.

All the same, she had missed her sister. Grisie had seemed so far away up there in the attic.

And now she was far away again, even when she lay beside Martha in the box bed at night, or sat beside her sewing, eating dinner, saying her prayers.

Duncan noticed it too, despite being away at school most of the day. He said all the fun had gone out of Grisie. "Fusses all the time, she does, worse than Mrs. MacFarlane down at the cottages," he complained to Martha. "She might as well be a hundred years auld as fifteen."

"Cook says all young ladies put on airs." Martha made a face. "She says it's natural as heather blooming."

"Well, *you'd* better not do it," Duncan said fiercely. "When you're fifteen, I'll be nearly eighteen—auld enough to shut you up in a closet and make you stay there until you come to your senses."

"I should hope you would, if ever I turned into an auld sourdook like Grisie," Martha declared. "Do you ken, she says I mustna say 'Mum' anymore? Told me it's a name for only bairns to use, she did, and that I'm too auld now for baby talk! We're to say 'Mother' now—or else 'Mama,' like French girls do. Only I'm not going to."

Duncan grimaced. "We ought to change *her* name from Grisie to Grannie."

Martha guffawed. Then Grisie came in and rolled her eyes heavenward as if asking the ceiling what could be done about a younger sister who made such unladylike noises. Martha, seeing it, laughed louder still.

It was one thing to laugh over Grisie's sulks with Duncan; it was quite another to endure them alone when he was at school. Mum never seemed to notice how cross Grisie was; she sang over her spinning and spun tales over her sewing, same as she had always done.

She sang:

Sour Grisie

"Tam o' the Linn came up the gate,
Wi' twenty puddings on a plate
And each pudding had a preen.
'We'll eat them all,' said Tam o' the Linn."

"What's a preen, Mum?" Martha interrupted.

"A dried plum, dear."

"It must have been a very big plate," said Martha thoughtfully, "if twenty puddings fit on it. Or else they were very wee puddings."

Grisie rolled her eyes. "It's only a song," she said. "It's nonsense. It isna meant to make sense."

Martha ignored her. She begged Mum to go on singing, and Mum did.

"Tam o' the Linn had no breeches to wear,
So he coft him a sheep's-skin to make him
*   a pair,*
The skinny side out, the woolly side in,
'It's grand summer clothin,' said
*   Tam o' the Linn.*

45

"Tam o' the Linn went over the moss,
To seek a stable for his horse:
The moss was open, and Tam fell in—
'I've stabled meself!' cried Tam o' the Linn."

Mum made a comical face when she sang Tam's part, and Martha laughed and laughed. She could not understand how Grisie kept from laughing, when Mum was being so funny. She wished for the thousandth time that Duncan did not have to go to school. *He* would not spoil things by keeping stonily silent.

A strange uncomfortable feeling rose up in Martha's soul, a naughty feeling of wanting to shout at Grisie or to—she hardly dared think it—to kick her. She knew she would never do those things, but she wanted to. And she knew the wanting to was almost as naughty as actually doing them would be. But her anger at Grisie's ill temper was fierce and terrible. It was not right that Grisie should be so sullen and snappish—not now, when Father had come home and the Stone House was growing lively again.

The Far Side o' the Hill

One morning Mum set Martha to work hemming and embroidering a set of handkerchiefs. There were four of the soft, thin squares of cloth. The edges of each one must be folded over exactly a quarter of an inch, pinned in place, and sewn with tiny perfect stitches all the way around. Then there were bits of yellow and crimson thread to stitch into a twining border of flowers whose centers were clusters of French knots. Mum showed Martha the pattern on a stitchery sampler and said the handkerchiefs would be good practice for her.

"I dinna understand," Martha said. "Canna we blow our noses just as well on plain handkerchiefs as on pretty ones?"

Mum smiled. "Aye, but it's pleasing to God when we strive to add beauty to the world, even in small ways. Besides, lass, it's meant to improve your sewing. I can see from your sampler that French knots are still getting the better of you."

Grisie, who was curled in Father's big armchair knitting lace, smiled over her needles. It would have been nice to see her smiling for once, if it had not been such a smug sort of smile. Grisie's French knots were everything a French knot could hope to be.

Martha made at face at her sister. French knots could stay in France, for all she cared.

All that morning she sat on her stool before the fire, laboring over the hem of the first handkerchief. The needle kept slipping and jabbing at her fingers. An endless road of tiny, maddening stitches stretched out before her—and at the end of it there would be the knots to tackle.

A bitter wind came rattling through the shutters and filling Mum's room with its chilly breath. Mollie entered and piled more peats on the fire. The April day was putting on a February face. Martha could not get comfortable. If she sat facing the fire, her cheeks burned but her back felt icy; and if she faced the other way, her fingers froze and her dress felt scorching hot against her back.

She kept turning around and around, until Grisie snapped at her. "Stop spinning, Martha! You're making me dizzy."

"You needna watch me," Martha retorted.

"How can I help it?" Grisie demanded. "You do it on purpose to distract me."

"I dinna!" Martha cried out.

"Martha!" Mum's voice was sharp.

"But—" Martha began, but Mum hushed her, sighed, and said Martha might go and play in the kitchen for a spell.

Gladly Martha sprang up from her stool, the handkerchief falling unmourned to the floor. She was itching to make a face at Grisie, but Mum was watching. So she ran as fast as she could out of the room and hurried down the narrow stone stairs to the kitchen, where Cook and Nannie bustled about preparing the noon meal, talking as fast as they worked.

The wind was just as busy at the kitchen shutters as it had been upstairs, and an icy draft came in from the hall. But in the enormous hearth golden coals glowed beneath bubbling kettles. Martha leaned against a pile of extra peats stacked against the wall, breathing in their good, grassy smell.

"Ah, here's Herself," said Cook. "I'd a notion we'd be seein' ye this mornin'. Mollie says it's all sour faces and pricked fingers upstairs."

Martha held up her fingers to show the sore tips. "Seven pricks, so far. And I've no even finished the first handkerchief." She sighed heavily.

Nannie, peeling potatoes over a bowl at the long kitchen worktable, clucked her tongue sympathetically. But Cook snorted and said, "Whisht! Who'd have thought Miss Martha Morse would be bested by somethin' as small and common as a needle? Afeared o' a wee bit o' sting, are ye?"

"I'm no afraid!" Martha flashed. "I can do it—I just dinna like it, that's all."

"Ah," said Cook, stirring her cauldron of broth, "that's a cat o' a different stripe. We most o' us has to do a good many things we dinna like. It's the way o' the world, lass. Here, measure me out two cups o' meal. Ye can help me make a skirl-in-the-pan for dinner, if *that* be to your likin'."

"Och, aye!" Martha jumped off the peat stack and snatched up the cup Cook used to measure out oatmeal and flour, and a bowl to pour it in. She went to the row of barrels that lined the kitchen wall beyond the peats and lifted off the lid of the oat barrel. Oatmeal puffed up and dusted her arms as she scooped and measured.

"Mind ye check it well for beetles," Cook said. "I found one in the barley yesterday. I dinna ken how we'll get through the summer, if the creepy-crawlies are this bad already."

"Ugh." Martha wrinkled her nose. She

hated the little black insects that invaded the kitchen and larder each summer. They got into the flour and the sugar and had to be picked out by hand.

But Martha did not see any beetles in the oatmeal today. She carried the bowl to Cook, who had just put a big three-legged skillet over a heap of coals to heat up.

Nannie's round face was thoughtful over her potatoes. She said, "Me mither says it's how ye go about doin' the jobs ye dinna like that counts. She says if ye're doin' something ye hate, but ye act like ye're havin' the time o' your life, why, soon ye'll find ye're not pretendin' after all—ye really are enjoying yourself."

Martha licked a bit of oatmeal dust off her arm. It was dry and gritty on her tongue. She was thinking about what Nannie had said. It made her think of Mollie, singing like a lark while she scrubbed the floors. Mollie had once admitted to Martha that she hated floor scrubbing more than any other chore. But to listen to her sing while scrubbing, you would think she was happy as could be.

"Your mither's a wise woman, Nannie Jenkins, and I've always been the first to say so," said Cook comfortably, dropping a hunk of fat into the skillet to melt. "That reminds me, did I hear aright that she's goin' up to the shieling this year? Mrs. Sandy was sayin' so."

"Aye," said Nannie. "Ma's goin' and takin' the whole brood wi' her, exceptin' me o' course. She says she's no spent a summer in the high country since the little ones was born, and she's bound to get there this year if she has to disguise herself as a cow."

Cook sent Martha to the larder for an onion and set to work chopping it into fine pieces with her big knife. Martha stood beside her watching, so close that the onion stung her eyes.

"I wish I could go to the shieling," she said.

The shieling was a place, high in the hills, where some of Father's tenants lived each summer in makeshift huts. They took Father's cattle up to the high meadows where grass was thick and plentiful, so that the pastures of the Glencaraid farm would not be over-grazed. Martha had heard many tales of the fun the cottagers had in the shieling—fiddling and dancing under the summer stars, toasting cheese over outdoor fires, picking flowers in hidden meadows that no one had set foot in for a year.

But Cook said, "It's no all fun and games, ye ken." She carried the chopped onions to the hearth and put them into the melted fat. They sizzled and hissed, and their savory smell filled the whole kitchen.

"It's a hard life away up there in the shieling," she said, "with the wind tearin' the thatch off your roof every third night, and everything smellin' o' cattle, and havin' to churn butter till your arms are like to fall off. It's twice as much work as a summer at home."

"I wouldna care," said Martha. "Anything would be better than sewing, and auld Grisie making a fuss about every little thing."

Cook and Nannie looked at each other.

"Och," said Cook wryly, "ye and your

sister are two peas in a pod."

"What?" Martha was outraged. "We're not a bit alike!"

Nannie was very busy with her potatoes, scraping the peels into a scrap pail.

"You've said so yourself, Cook—many a time," Martha persisted. Cook's mouth twitched and her sharp eyes met Martha's.

"Happen I have. Sometimes, lassie, truth wears one hat, and sometimes it wears another."

Martha didn't have the least idea what Cook was talking about. She rolled her eyes, exasperated, and then the image came to her of Grisie rolling *her* eyes about something Martha had said. She stood stock-still a moment, feeling a little uncomfortable. Perhaps—perhaps Cook wasn't talking nonsense after all. But she said stubbornly, "Grisie wouldna go to the shieling for all the gold in Scotland. She'd hate it there, and I wouldna. I'd love it."

"True," said Cook. "But ye're both ailin' from the selfsame thing—always wishin' to be something ye're not. The grass is ever greener on the far side o' the hill, that's what."

"What does Grisie want?"

"Och, that one! Got her head all filled up wi' fancy notions, she did, when yer cousins were visitin'. Now her nose is out o' joint because yer Father willna send her away to their school for fine young ladies in Edinburgh."

"Grisie wants to go away?" Martha could not believe her ears. "She'd never!"

"Hush, child, dinna shout," Cook scolded. "Ye'll have her down here givin' us a piece o' her mind for talkin' about her business. There, now, me onions are nice an' brown."

Slowly she poured in the ground oats, stirring them into the melted fat and sizzling onions.

"It was your cousin Janet, that's who," she went on, "who filled Grisie's head with talk about that foolishness they teach them in the boarding school—French, and dancing, and fine needlework. As if your sister needs anyone to show her how to hauld a needle! There's no a lass in the county can outstitch Miss Grisie. Och, and they study drawin', and fan

paintin', and sculptin' apples and plums out
o' wax, and other such useful accomplish-
ments."

She snorted, to show what she thought of
a school that prided itself on its pupils' abil-
ity to make wax fruit. Martha thought it
sounded awful; she could not imagine wish-
ing to attend a school of that sort. And here
was Cook saying it was for want of this school
that Grisie had become so sour and broody!

Cook's long-handled spoon went round and
round the skillet, stirring the oatmeal mixture.
The skirl-in-the-pan was thick as paste now,
with fat bubbles of air rising to the surface
and lazily popping. Cook salted and peppered
it and took it off the coals.

"Mmm," Martha said. She was suddenly
very hungry. The potatoes were boiling in a
kettle of water, and Nannie was slicing up
some salted beef.

A ripple of music drifted out of the parlor:
Grisie had come downstairs to play the pianoforte. Martha went softly across the hall to the
parlor and stood in the doorway, listening.

The pianoforte was near the door, facing into the room, as far from the fireplace as possible. Grisie had her back to Martha. She sat very straight, her dark glossy head tilted to one side. Her hair was coiled in a low knot, with little tendrils curling on her neck. The smooth neat row of black keys stretched out on either side of her, with the ivory keys between the black ones shining like pearls.

Martha dutifully practiced her *Hook's* every day, but she could not play like this. Grisie's hands fluttered lightly as birds back and forth across the keys. The music was like a live thing.

To think Grisie wanted to go away and live in the city and play the pianoforte for a bunch of silly girls at school instead of for her own family! Martha felt again that terrible urge to kick her—how could Grisie think of such a thing? And yet part of Martha was wanting to run up and throw her arms around her sister and squeeze her tight. It was bad enough that Alisdair and Robbie had been sent away. Probably Duncan would be sent away also, in a year or two. Grisie was the only one who would not have to leave, ever, unless she wanted to.

Martha stood there a long time, listening. Grisie was playing a song that she had learned last fall, at the same time that Martha was learning to spin on a drop spindle. Grisie had played the tune over and over while Martha practiced spinning as she walked. Hearing the music now brought the tingling feeling of spinning to Martha's fingertips. Spinning meant wool, and wool meant sheepshearing, and that meant spring. The loveliest parts of spring were just around the corner now—clover honey, the crisp fresh taste of watercress, the smell of heather. It was like magic, the way Grisie could play a feeling right into someone's head. It was such a very different feeling from the one she had bored into Martha with her disdainful eyes, up in Mum's room!

Handsome Is as Handsome Does

Spring arrived in earnest at last. It was plain to Martha that the sun felt about springtime as she did, for it climbed out of bed earlier each morning and lingered in the evening sky a little longer each night. She wished she could be like the sun, watching everything at once. Or like the wind, racing from one corner of the valley to the next, whisking down to help scatter grain in the plowed fields or to tickle the ears of the large-eyed lambs that followed their mothers in the meadows. There was so much to see every day, a thousand things happening all over Father's estate, and every one of them interesting. She did not want to miss a single one.

One warm day all the Glencaraid sheep were herded to a stream at the bottom of the valley. Martha coaxed Mum into letting her go and watch. Perched on a heathery hillock overlooking the stream, she cheered as the men pushed the sheep into the water and held them still with straining arms. It was a sort of contest between men and sheep. The sheep did not want to be bathed, but they must be before they were shorn.

Martha would have liked to help. The noisy blatting of the sheep, the splashing and tussling—all of it was like a drink of water after a long thirst. It was lovely to know that the outdoor time of year had come at last.

The men scrubbed the sheep, rubbing the fluffy wool until all the year's muck and dust had been scrubbed away and the wool was clean and creamy white. A great cloud of dirt and oil floated away downstream of the scrubbed sheep. The oil glistened on the water and cast rainbows that quivered in the ripples. The hands of the scrubbing men glistened too, from the grease that made sheep's wool so springy and absorbent.

The crofters waited five or six days for the sheep to dry. Then the shearing began—a noisy, bustling process that took the better part of a day. A man would catch a sheep and pin it down with one leg, and with big metal shears he would cut off the sheep's wool. He began close to the sheep's body, under one of the front legs, and clipped the crinkly wool close to the skin. Then, working his way around to the neck and face, he carefully snipped away the wool there. The shearing did not hurt the sheep, though they hated to be pinned down.

Shearing around the head was the slow part. When the man got to the sheep's back, he cut very quickly. A good shearer could slide the shears right along the sheep's skin, clipping rapidly without ever once nicking the sheep's skin.

The curly ends of the wool clung together, so the fleece came off the sheep's body all in one piece. Then the fleece was ready for Mum and Grisie and Mollie to comb it and prepare it for spinning.

But just now Mum was more occupied with last year's fleeces, which had already been spun into woolen yarn. Every spare minute during the long winter, Mum and Grisie and the maids had spun and spun. Martha had spun a lot of wool herself, on her drop spindle.

And when all the wool was spun, there had been the linen to do. Linen was a finer, stiffer thread that came from the crushed stalks of flax plants. Mum liked wool for winter clothing and blankets, and linen for lighter clothing and for sheets and tablecloths and napkins. Martha had not yet learned to spin flax into linen. That was trickier, and took more practice.

Now, with winter past, the time had come to dye the yarn, both wool and linen, and to send it to the webster in Clachan, the little village across Loch Caraid. Mr. Cameron would weave the yarn into cloth on his looms. Martha knew what a loom was, but she had never seen one. She had never been inside the webster's shop. It seemed the greatest mystery to her how on earth Mr. Cameron managed to take all those skeins of yarn, the soft heaps of them nestled in baskets like a litter of kittens curled one on top another, and turn them into bolts of cloth.

A few weeks after the sheepshearing, Mr. Cameron's two oldest sons delivered the long, rolled-up bolt of woolen cloth. The sons unrolled the cloth on the parlor table and waited while Mum looked it over. She inspected the edges to see that they were neat and even; she checked the plaid pattern. She took handfuls of cloth and scrunched it together and spread it out, and felt its weight on her hands.

Mr. Cameron's sons stood patiently watching. They were stout, ruddy young men with thick unruly masses of hair; one of them had a homely face and the other was strong jawed and handsome. Martha had seen them in church, and she knew they had a younger brother, Ian, who was at school with Duncan. She knew, too, for Cook had said so just yesterday, that the handsome one, Henry, was bound for Glasgow as soon as he came of age. He hoped to make a fortune in the cotton trade.

"The more fool he," Cook had said, snorting, "givin' up a good place here in his father's shop, for who kens what in some grimy corner o' the city. He'll come to ruin, that one, for he hasna the good sense o' a sheep. His brother Gerald, now, he's the clever one, and a good kindhearted lad too. A pity he's so ill favored."

"Handsome is as handsome does, me mither always says," Nannie had responded pertly, and Cook's eyebrows had twitched in a knowing kind of way.

Martha had watched this exchange with great interest. She knew there was something more to what Cook and Nannie were saying that went beyond the words they spoke out loud. Now, while Mum inspected the cloth, Martha stared at Gerald, studying his face. He had rough skin, a jutting nose, and rather pouchy eyes. But there was a kind light shining out from the eyes, and he smiled at Martha in the friendliest way. She smiled back at him and at his brother. Henry did not seem to notice Martha was there. He shifted restlessly from foot to foot, waiting for Mum to speak.

At last Mum looked up and said she was well pleased with the cloth.

Martha turned her gaze back to the fabric. She felt even more pleased with it than Mum was. When she looked at the bright bands of color running across the fabric, wide red ones and thinner black ones, and narrow ribbons of white-yellow-white running between them, like streaks of light, she felt a queer feeling in her middle. There was something so exactly *right* about the the neat, lively rows. They fit together like stones in a wall, or like twigs laced together in a bird's nest.

Martha stared at the colors so long that when she looked away, she saw a kind of ghost plaid on the wall. Then she blinked and the ghosts went away. She stared hard at the cloth again and made a game of seeing the ghostly stripes on the floor, on her dust-gown, even on Mum's face.

Mum paid the young men and said they must be sure to stop in the kitchen for a bite to eat before they headed back to the village. Martha followed them, to see just what sort of a bite they would be given. There was always the possibility Cook would be handing out slices of pie.

Gerald and Henry called out greetings to Nannie and Cook. Nannie came forward with bread and cheese for the two young men. Martha sighed: no pie after all. Nannie served the men shyly, her pretty rosy face gone rather pale. Handsome Henry smiled winningly at her and said he hoped she had made the bread herself.

"It's sure to be sweeter than cake if those pretty hands have touched it," he teased. Nannie drew back, flustered; her color came rushing back all at once. Martha stared at her curiously.

Nannie murmured, "Ye'll want a sip o' ale

wi' that," and went quickly to the larder, frowning. Gerald gave his brother a sideways look with a little shake of the head; but Henry only grinned.

When Nannie brought the mugs of ale, she did not lift her eyes to look at the young men. Henry did not tease her anymore. He grabbed for his mug and said a hearty "Ah, *much* obliged" that seemed directed more to the ale mug than to Nannie.

Gerald thanked her softly. Nannie's cheeks were rosier than ever.

Henry drained his mug of ale and asked Nannie if he couldn't trouble her for another drop. He gave Nannie another of his winning smiles and even made so bold as to wink at her. Martha saw Nannie frown again, and at the hearth Cook's spoon was very loud in her kettle.

Clearing his throat nervously, Gerald remarked about how fine the fishing had been lately. Nannie was just opening her mouth in reply when Henry suddenly exclaimed sharply and spit out a bite of cheese.

"Faugh! What's this? A beetle!" His ruddy face was crinkled in disgust. "Fine fare for the laird's own kitchen! Canna ye serve me better than this, lass?"

Nannie shrank back in horror and shame. Cook came roaring up to see, and she kicked at the little black bug with an outraged foot.

"Ye needna make such a stink aboot it," she snapped at the young man. "We've been plagued wi' beetles these two years past, same as every househauld in the valley. If there's aught can rid a hoose o' them, it's yet to be discovered."

Henry looked over the rest of his cheese suspiciously; his eyes upon Nannie were scornful. Martha wanted to kick him.

"Hedgehog," said Gerald suddenly. Everyone looked at him in surprise.

He gave a lopsided grin and explained. "Get yourselves a hedgehog to keep in the kitchen. Hedgers eat beetles—think they're kings' food, they do. Ye can give it a box o' straw to sleep in, and let it roam about as it likes."

"Aye, let's do!" Martha cried, clapping her hands. To think of having your own little spiny black-eyed hedgehog living in your very house! She could feed it cream from a saucer and bring it fresh straw for its little bed.

"But where will we get one?" she asked. Gerald squatted down beside her and said he had an idea or two how one could be found.

"Ye'll want a young one," he said, "so it'll grow up thinkin' it aye belongs wi' people. Ye just leave it to me, miss; I shall no leave ye wantin'." He smiled at her. Nannie's smile shone down on him, but he did not look up to see it.

Martha saw it, though. She had noticed a great many things in the kitchen today, and her mind was swimming with questions. She had scarcely ever seen anything so interesting as all these strange smiles and frowns and blushes. But the thought of a hedgehog coming to live in the Stone House was more interesting still. When Henry had noisily emptied his second mug of ale and the two young men had gone on their way down the hill, Martha ran back into the parlor to tell Mum about the hedgehog.

Mum was still looking at the cloth outspread upon the parlor table. She said she thought a hedgehog was a grand notion; the beetles had been such a problem last year and would only get worse as summer came on.

Martha leaned over the cloth, smelling its woolly scent. The golden stripes were so bright they seemed to float above the surface of the cloth, like sunlight shining on the lake. Martha ran her fingers along them; the cloth was stiff and scratchy—wool always was until it had been fulled properly. It must be waulked to make it soft and thick and warm, and that meant it was time for a waulking.

Waulking the Wool

Beside the Stone House, at the foot
of the green mountain that rose up
beyond the garden wall, there was a
wide, smooth stretch of ground. This was
where the waulking was always done. On a
clear morning Sandy and his son Neil carried
Mum's woolen cloth there and unrolled it upon
the clean grass.

Almost all the women of Glencaraid came
for the waulking. The wives of the crofters
came, and their older daughters, to do the
work. The grandmothers came, to help with

the singing and to look after the babies. Nannie and Mollie left their work in the Stone House for one morning. Only Cook did not come, for the laird's dinner must be made, waulking or no.

Auld Mary came too, though she did not have to. Auld Mary was the wise woman who lived alone out on the moor, in a tiny one-room hut filled with dried herbs and potions. She was a healer; anyone who was sick sent for Auld Mary, and she came with a cure tucked in her apron. Hyacinth roots chopped and fried in butter for getting rid of boils; barberry bark for jaundice; tincture of celandine to soothe itching eyes. She delivered all the babies who were born in the valley, and when someone died Auld Mary came to help lay out the body for the funeral. She had an orange cat with white paws, to whom she spoke as if it were a person and could understand her. People said the cat talked back to Auld Mary. Martha had met the cat, and she believed it.

From the bedroom window, where she sat

putting agonized stitches into one of her handkerchiefs, Martha watched Auld Mary's bent
shape toiling up the hill toward the waulking
place. Martha longed to run out and join her,
but Mum said that Martha must finish her
day's sewing first.

"Could I not take it with me?" Martha
begged, and Mum's merry laugh pealed across
the room.

"So it can get trampled on where you've
flung it onto the grass and forgotten it? Aye,
I ken well how much sewing you're likely to
do out there wi' all those goings-on to stick
your nose into. Nay, my lass, duty first—then
fun."

So Martha hurried as best she could to finish the hem. She was determined not to miss
anything. The women would sing, and the
children would play games, and Auld Mary
would tell a story. She told marvelous stories.
The second Mum set her free, Martha bolted
down the stairs, out the front door, and around
the side of the house. The air was sweet with
the perfume of the purple heather blossoms

that blanketed the hillsides all around.

The women were already settling into their places around the waulking-boards. These were flat pieces of wood with narrow grooves cut into them lengthwise, so that each board was ridged all over like a washboard. They were laid end to end, to form one long row on the grass. Spread upon the boards was the long roll of fabric, which had first been soaked well with clean water.

The wet cloth was dark and heavy, its colors dulled. When it dried, the colors would be bright as ever, but the cloth would be wholly different. The water would shrink it; and the women would make it soft and pliable by working it with their feet against the grooved waulking-boards.

They sat on the grass facing each other. Half the women sat on one side of the cloth and half on the other, with their skirts hiked up to the knee and their bare feet outstretched upon the cloth. Auld Mary's knees cracked as she lowered herself to her place. She was older than the oldest grandmother who had come to watch, but she always joined the waulkers for the first song. Her black eyes twinkled out at Martha beneath her yellowed linen cap.

Martha waved at her. She was glad to see Auld Mary.

Mrs. Sandy, the wife of Father's steward, knelt at the far end with an upturned kettle and a sturdy wooden spoon, where the head of the table would be if the women were seated around a table instead of along a bolt of cloth. She was going to be the leader—Mrs. Sandy was always the leader at a waulking. She kept good time and sang so authoritatively that no one could ever dare to lag behind the pace she had set.

Singing was an important part of the waulking, Martha knew—perhaps the most important. It was one of the things she liked best about it. The truth was, a waulking was a great deal more fun for the children watching than for the women working. The waulkers would have to push and beat the wool with their feet for a very long time, all in the same rhythm.

If anyone fell out of rhythm, her section of the wool would shrink a different amount than the rest of the cloth. The finished cloth would be buckled and imperfect.

If a waulker worked too fast or beat too hard, the wool might be felted—the separate fibers would knot together in a tight, fuzzy mat. The cloth would be too thick and dense for Mum to make clothing out of it. It would have to become a blanket, and not a very good one at that.

But there was no fear of that happening, because Mrs. Sandy was in charge, and because all the women—Auld Mary, Nannie, Mollie; young Mrs. Tervish, who had had a baby last year and had named him Allan in honor of Father; the other wives and the grown-up daughters of the farmers who worked Father's land—knew what they were doing. They had done it many, many times before. They would do it again, many more times.

Mrs. Sandy sat upright on her heels, hands on hips, surveying the assembled women with a sharp eye.

Martha felt it was a very glad sort of day. There was an exciting tension in the air as the women prepared to start. She danced from one foot to the other. Mrs. Sandy raised her spoon; she brought it down on the kettle with a dull clang; she began to sing.

"One day I was walkin' the hills.
Heavy rain and mist came upon us.
A boat was seen at sea, comin'.
If there was anyone on it, my dearest was,
My love John, me darlin' Roderick."

It was an old waulking song, and it was not like any other kind of music. Each line wrapped into the next without stopping; the verses flowed one into the other with no pause for breath or emphasis. The steady, even beat must never falter.

The women sang and their feet pushed and pulled the cloth across the ridged boards. Mrs. Sandy's arm moved up and down beating the kettle, as regular as a clock. Mollie's sweet voice, higher than the others, lifted the melody to the sky. Beside her Auld Mary crooned in her low, rough voice that seemed as old as a mountain.

"If he was to come near the fold,
Water from the spring wouldna be his drink
But milk from the best cow in the fold,
from the yellow one, and the brun."

The sky and the steep green hills were listening. *Scritch, scratch* went the moving feet and the whispering cloth.

Birds sang in the gorse bushes, and it seemed they were trying to sing the waulking song. The older women who sat knitting or doing their mending on the sweet-smelling grass sang also, when they were not scolding the two- and three- and four-year-olds who had been brought along to play while their mothers and sisters worked.

Baby Allan Tervish shouted and crawled in the grass, half hidden by pink-budded stems of clover. Sometimes he sat down hard on his little cloth-wrapped bottom and waved his arms in the air, as if he were Mrs. Sandy without the spoon and kettle. He tried to crawl onto the waulking-boards and the wet cloth, but Martha ran forward and hauled him away. This made him scream with laughter. He knew Martha well, for she often went down to his cottage to visit.

When she let him go, he tried again to crawl onto the cloth. He wore a determined baby grin; he thought it was a game. Martha and the other children took turns dragging him backward by his chubby legs, to hear his funny chortling laugh. As soon as he was let go, he scrambled forward as fast as he could, and then he would stop and peek over his shoulder to see who was coming to get him. Martha and the children, and the grandmothers too, were all laughing so hard they could not sing anymore.

The waulking women never stopped working for an instant. But their eyes were laughing as they watched the baby's antics.

When the song was over, Auld Mary rose

to her feet. Quickly another woman slipped into her place. Mrs. Sandy raised her spoon and brought it down hard on the kettle: a new song was begun.

The Laird's Lass and
the Smith's Son

At the edge of the waulking place grew a stubby, wind-twisted old pine. Auld Mary went to rest in its patchy shade. The children clustered round her; Martha scooped up little Allan under his arms and carried him over. Auld Mary's stories were an important part of a waulking. Father said there was not a storyteller like her in all the county—not even Mum, and that was saying a lot.

Auld Mary looked at the little crowd of children and pretended to be perplexed. Behind the children the waulking song beat steadily on above the cloth.

"Canna an auld woman take a wee rest withoot all the bairns o' Glencaraid comin' to gawp at her?"

Her black eyes sparkled at them. In her faded gray skirt and dull-green shawl, Auld Mary was like an old pine tree herself, bent and weathered by the mountain winds.

"Give us a tale!" Martha cried, and the smaller children echoed her.

"Aye, Auld Mary, give us a tale! Please, please!"

Auld Mary looked from face to face and cackled; her bent shoulders shook.

She winked at Martha and said, "So, Mouse, I see it's a tribe o' mice ye've found yerself. Me auld Kitty'll be that sorry he missed the fun."

Martha was very pleased. Auld Mary remembered the nickname she had given Martha many months ago. It was something, having a special name that only Auld Mary called you.

"Aye, then," Auld Mary went on, "I can see there's naught for it but to give ye scamps yer tale. Ye must pay a forfeit, though—let's see, what shall it be? A nose from each o' ye? An ear?"

Her dark eyes darted around the circle again, and the children made little shuffling movements. They all knew Auld Mary well— hadn't she been present when every one of them was born?—and they loved her, but she frightened them a little nonetheless. Some folks said Auld Mary was a witch; even Martha's own mother said the old woman had the second sight. Auld Mary knew things without being told. She knew most everything there was to know, it seemed.

But Martha was not afraid of her, not anymore. She had been, when she was as small as little Nelly Jenkins and Hugh Davis. Martha was a big girl of seven now, and she knew when Auld Mary was teasing.

"Nay," she laughed. "Not our noses, nor our ears neither."

"Attached to them, are ye?" said Auld Mary. "One nose, then; and ye shall choose atween ye whose it's to be."

Now all the children laughed. "Nay!" they cried.

"Ah," said Auld Mary, "then there shall be nae tale. I must have a nose—a tiny wee one will do. Or else I'll no speak a word about the lass who woke up one mornin' wi' a dog's head on her shoulders."

The children clamored; now they *must* have the tale, for there could be no peace for any of them until they found out who the lass was and why she had the head of a dog instead of her own girl's head.

Martha bit her lip, thinking hard. Auld Mary didn't really want a nose, but she did want something; it was like a riddle.

"Hold still, Allan," Martha said, shifting the fidgety baby on her lap. His small hands grabbed at her face, and suddenly she cried out. "Can the wee nose stay on its face?"

Auld Mary clapped her hands together sharply, beaming.

"Clever lass! Aye, that's just the sort o' snub liddle nose I'm after," she said, and she opened her arms for baby Allan. Martha settled him on Auld Mary's lap. The baby, whom Martha had never known to do anything but wriggle and poke and squirm, sat perfectly still in the old woman's arms, staring up gravely at her wrinkled face.

Auld Mary chuckled softly and touched the baby's nose with the tip of a finger. She said, "Noo then. We shall have our bit o' a tale."

The children sat hushed, and behind them the waulking women sang steadily on while Auld Mary told her story.

There once was a laird, and he had a daughter. Aye, a bonny thing she was, and a clever one too. And when she got to be a young lady, the laird put his mind to findin' her a husband. After looking over this young man and that one, he settled on a handsome young earl from the next county. This earl, he had a castle and hounds and a horse that was the envy o'

every man who saw him. The laird thought
he was just the sort o' fellow who'd make
a fine son-in-law, and he told his wife he'd
found a man for their daughter to wed.
Och, the girl's mother was well pleased,
and she set to sewin' the bridal clothes
right away.

But when the lass got wind o' it, ye can
be certain she had her own ideas on the
subject. She kenned the earl was well
enough to look at, and no one could argue
that he had not a fine castle and a finer
horse.

But she kenned also that the earl was a
proud and cruel sort o' man. She had heard
all about him from her maid, who had a
sister in the earl's castle. Aye, and the
maid's sister had told fearful stories o' how
the earl behaved when something dis-
pleased him—rantin' and shoutin' and
shuttin' people up in dark closets.

The lass tried to tell her father some o'
this, but he waved it off as servants' gos-
sip. And the lass, she didna blame her

father, for she kenned that he loved her well and truly sought to make a happy match for her. "It was no his fault that the earl was a double-hearted sort o' man, who put on an agreeable face when there was something he wanted, and only showed his true colors after he had gotten it.

Nay, the lass didna fault her father, but she kenned she couldna marry the terrible earl. She went up to her room to think the matter over, and she decided there was only one thing she could do.

"If it's a husband they want for me, it's a husband I'll find," said the lass to herself. "But he must be good and kind and honest. I'd sooner live in a kennel with the dogs than marry a man like the earl. Now—where to start lookin', that's the main thing."

She thought over all the young men who'd ivver been guests in her father's castle. Not a one o' them jumped out at her as the sort o' man she'd like to marry. It wasna long before the lass decided she'd have to go out in the world to look for a husband, and she kenned a young lady of her station would nivver get far on her own without people askin' questions. So she slipped into the servants' quarters and borrowed the dairymaid's Sunday gown.

"Now then," she said to herself, tuckin' her pretty hair up under the dairymaid's bonnet, "I'd best be startin'. I expect it's a fool's quest I'm on, but ah, well. A goin' foot will aye get something, if it's nothin' but a thorn or a broken toe."

She left her father's grounds and walked right into the village. She was lookin' about, makin' up her mind whether to go this way or that, when suddenly she spied a lad comin' toward her on the road. A tall, fine-lookin' fellow, he was, with a swingin' stride and a strong chin. The lass, she took a fancy to him at once.

But she saw that he wore a leather apron and carried a hammer in his hand, and the lass said to herself, "Och, I mustna fall for this lad—he's naught but a blacksmith, if I'm no mistaken."

And she was no mistaken, for the lad was the son of the village smith. He kept on comin' down the road toward the lass, and she saw that he had a kind face and a clever eye.

Then she had another thought, and it bein', *Why* shouldna *I wed a smith if I want to? If he's the one for me, then he's the one, and that's that. But I'll nivver ken for sure just from gawpin' at him.*

So she determined to have a word with the lad. As he drew near, she made bold to speak to him, and he answered her in the friendliest, most courteous manner. She asked him if he could tell her where to find the mill, and he said that as he was goin' that way himself, he'd be glad to take her there.

"Ye must be newly arrived to this area," said the lad politely, "for ye were goin' quite the wrong direction."

The lass said that she'd lived all her life in the house o' the laird, and didna very often leave the grounds. And that was the truth, too, though the lad had no notion it was the laird's own daughter he was speakin' to.

All the way to the mill the lad and the lass talked and laughed together. By the time they reached it, the lass had quite made up her mind that this kind, clever, lighthearted lad was indeed the lad for her. And as for the lad, he was thinkin' the same thing about the lassie, and wonderin' how it was he'd nivver seen her before in all the times he'd been out to the laird's castle. Sure and she had a familiar look, he thought, and he said to himself that happen he'd passed her in the courtyard once or twice as she went about her work in the laird's dairy. (For he thought from her frock and bonnet that she was a dairy-maid, ye recall.)

Well, the lass waited until the lad had finished at the mill and gone back on his way to the smithy, and then she turned herself around and went home. She crept up the back stairs and put on her own clothes, and she slipped the dairymaid's gown and bonnet back into her room.

After that there was many a day when the laird's lass borrowed those clothes and slipped away to the village to spend a few minutes talkin' to the blacksmith's son. He, for his part, was ivver glad to see her, though he did wonder from time to time how it was that a dairymaid had so many errands in the village. But his heart fair split in two each time he bid her good-bye, and it wasna long before he began to talk o' one day makin' her a home.

Things went on this way for a piece, and then one day at dinner the laird announced that he'd set a wedding date for his daughter and the young earl. The lass, she turned pale, and she said, "I'm sorry, Father, but I canna marry the earl. There's only one lad for me, and him the blacksmith's son."

Och, ye can imagine the uproar that followed. The laird roared and the lady cried, and the lass's bonny eyes that had always been so smilin' and happy were filled with terrible grief. In the end the laird said he didna ken what to do with the girl, and he sent her up to her chambers to wait until he did.

The next day, the laird said the lass must marry the earl, like it or no. He said he'd sent for the earl that very mornin', and the two were to be wed on the morrow.

When the lass was left alone once more, she set to thinkin' up a way out of her predicament. She had to find a way to show her father the earl's true colors, so that he would see that the earl was not at all the kind of man he wanted his daughter to marry. Then, too, she must find a way to make him see that the blacksmith's son *was*.

She thought and she thought and she spent the whole day thinking. Evening came, and she still had not thought of an answer to the problem. The only thing she could think of was to go away, and not marry either one.

So that night she crept out of the castle

and made her way through the wood
behind the gardens. She didna go toward
the village this time, for she didna want to
be seen. She walked a long way through
the woods, scratchin' herself on brambles
and gettin' her feet all cold and wet crossin'
brooks, until she was near faintin' with
weariness. And just when she thought she
couldna take one step more, she saw a
little house through the trees. And when
she came closer, she saw that it wasna a
house at all, but an auld kirk, with the
moon shining over its steeple.

The lass, she was that thankful she
almost wept. She stumbled into the kirk
and sank down on one o' the benches. She
was just sinkin' into sleep when she heard
two voices talkin'.

"Isna that the laird's daughter?" said the
first voice, and a tiny wee squeakin' sort
o' voice it was. The lass looked all around,
but she couldna see who was speakin'.

"Aye," said the second voice, and it was
tinier and squeakier than the first. "It's her,

poor lass, the very one the sparrows were tellin' us about. It's all over the wood, what's goin' on at the castle."

The lass called out then and asked who it was who was talkin', and where were they? But no one answered her. There was only a little scurryin' sound near the front o' the kirk, and she looked and saw two wee brown mice peekin' out from behind the altar. After a moment she heard the first voice say:

"Och, she's awake! Sure and she frightened me. But I'd go to her in a minute, if only she spoke a bit o' Mouse. I'd tell her I ken just how she might solve her problem."

Then the lass understood that the voices she heard belonged to the mice! She wanted to cry out that she *did* hear what they were sayin'—but she realized she couldna speak in the mouse tongue. And she didna ken how she could understand it, either. But there was no denyin' she did understand, and this is what she heard:

The second mouse was saying to the first mouse, "Ah, is it fern seeds ye're thinkin' of?"

And the first mouse answered, "Nay, I dinna ken as turnin' invisible would help her at all. Anyway, midnight was an hour gone. Fern seeds has got to be harvested at the stroke o' twelve, or the magic willna work."

"Och, aye," said the second mouse, twitchin' its whiskers, "I was forgettin' that."

"It's dog's violet I'm thinkin' of," the first mouse said. "If only the lass would look under the elm tree in front o' the kirk, she'd find a patch o' dog's violet that came up after the rain that fell last Midsummer's Eve. A few o' its leaves chewed up and swallowed would set her right."

"Ah, I see what ye're gettin' at. Only the tears o' a good man could break the spell," said the second mouse. "Aye, it's a clever mouse ye are. It would be the very thing. So long as the lass didna mind—"

But what the lass might mind she was not to hear, for just then the wind caught the kirk door and banged it against the wall, and it startled her so that she cried out. The two mice darted into a mousehole. The lass took out the bit o' cheese she had tucked into her pocket, and she laid it on the floor near the mousehole. Then she left the kirk and found the old elm tree and the dog's violet underneath. She plucked a few leaves and worrited them down (and terrible bitter-tastin' they were, too), and then she hurried back through the woods toward her home.

When she got home, she washed her face and went to bed. The next mornin' she woke up in a fright, as well she might, for her maid was standin' beside the bed screamin' her head off.

The lass's mother came runnin' in, and she screamed too. That brought the laird runnin', and he screamed loudest of all. It was a long while before everyone stopped carryin' on long enough for the lass to find out what all the screamin' was about. But when she found out, she felt like screamin' herself.

For the long and short of it is, the dog's-violet leaves had turned her own pretty head into the head of a hound.

To be sure, it was the head o' a handsome dog, with glossy brown fur and big melting brown eyes. But even the finest-looking dog's head is a frightful thing to see upon a human body. Och, the lass, she was a sight, with her little pale hands feeling around the soft fur and the wet nose and the big floppin' ears.

For a moment or two the lass bitterly regretted followin' the mice's advice. But then she recalled how earnestly concerned the mice had been, and she kenned they would no have a dog's head in mind as a permanent end to her problem. Trustin' the kirkmice had got her this far, and she decided to go right on trustin' them.

So she said to her father, "I'm sorry to

have caused ye any worry, sir, and that's the truth. I've eaten somethin' as doesna quite agree with me, but I'm in no pain, and I'm same lass I ivver was. I'm ready now to marry the earl, if he'll have me."

For she remembered that the mice had said only a good man could break the spell. The lass had a good head on her shoulders—even if it was a dog's—and she had figured out a thing or two. She had an idea the earl wouldna take kindly to this turn o' events.

While all the fuss and uproar was goin' on upstairs, the earl had arrived and was waitin' in the main parlor. The laird didna ken what else to do but have his daughter put on her best gown and go down to greet her bridegroom.

The earl, he took one look at at the dog-headed lass, and he screamed. He took a second look at her and scrambled for the door. He took a third look and turned purple with rage, and he shouted that the laird had tricked him and they ought all to be shut up in dark closets for the rest o' their lives.

And that was the last the laird's family ivver saw o' the earl.

Then the lass said again what she had told her father the day before—that she wanted to marry the blacksmith's son.

"What makes ye think he'll not run screamin' too?" said the laird.

"Happen he will," the lass answered. "We'll not know unless we try him."

And so the laird sent a man to fetch the blacksmith's son. The servant didna mention the dog's head—he told the lad only that the laird wanted to see him about his daughter, whom he'd been courtin'. When the lad heard that the lass he'd thought was a dairymaid was truly the laird's daughter, he near fell into his forge. He thought it likely the laird had summoned him to have him thrown into prison. But the blacksmith's son was a brave lad, and he went to the castle at once.

When he arrived, he near fell over again,

for the laird came to him at once and clapped him on the back, and said the lad was welcome to marry his daughter if that was what he wanted.

And then the lad had a third shock, for he looked at the lass and saw the dog's head where her own bonny head ought to have been.

She explained about eatin' something that put a spell on her, and told him she'd understand if he'd changed his mind about marryin' her.

Tears sprang to the lad's eyes as he stepped forward and caught her up in his arms. "I loved ye when I thought ye were a dairymaid," he said, "and I loved ye still when I found out ye were the laird's daughter and I'd likely go to prison for courtin' ye. I'll not stop lovin' ye now, just because your bonny wee face has grown a bit o' fur."

He hugged her close, and his tears fell upon her cheeks, and—what do ye suppose? Just like that, the dog's head was gone and the lass's own bonny face was smilin' up at him. And the laird and his lady saw that the blacksmith's lad was a fine, good-hearted man, and they considered themselves right lucky to have him for a son-in-law. The lass and the lad were married, and the laird made the lad steward over all his lands, and they all lived happily all the days o' their lives.

Auld Mary finished her story and looked around at the children. Baby Allan was asleep in her lap. Martha sat very still, hugging her knees.

"Even the mice?" she asked.

"Especially the mice," Auld Mary replied. "Ye see, after that the lass nivver would let anyone set a trap anywhere on her father's land. She made a rule that a portion o' grain from every harvest was to be left for the mice—and the mice returned the favor by leavin' the househauld stores alone. So it was a good end all 'round."

Father Tells His Secret

What with the waulking, and the promise of the hedgehog, and all her work on the handkerchiefs, Martha had quite forgotten about the secret Father was keeping. He hadn't mentioned it since the day after he came home from his trip.

But a day or two after the waulking, he came out of the house with a letter in his hands and a twinkle in his eye. Martha was prowling along the house wall looking at the ferns that grew in curly-fronded clusters against the stones, while Mum sat singing on the heather bench with a bit of needlework in her hands.

"O, you'll take the high road, and I'll take the low road,
And I'll be in Scotland afore ye;
But me and my true love will never meet again
On the bonnie, bonnie banks o' Loch Lomond."

The heather bench was a low seat made of earth built against the front wall of the Stone House, upon which a thick blanket of heather bloomed soft and purple. There was hardly a pleasanter spot in all of Glencaraid, there with the Stone House at your back and the sweet fragrance of heather all around, and Loch Caraid glittering at the bottom of the hill before you.

Father sat down next to Mum and stretched his long legs out in front of him. His deep voice picked up the thread of Mum's song—

"The wee birdies sing and the wild flowers
   spring,
And in sunshine the waters are sleeping;
But the broken heart it kens no second spring,
Tho' the woeful may cease from their greeting.

"O, you'll take the high road, and I'll take the
   low road,
And I'll be in Scotland afore ye;
But me and my true love will never meet
   again
On the bonnie, bonnie banks o' Loch Lomond."

Martha listened to them while she inspected the undersides of the fern leaves. She was thinking about what the mice in Auld Mary's story had said about fern seeds collected at midnight having the power to make a person invisible. Martha could think of a great many things she would like to do that would be easier if no one could see her. She would follow Duncan to school and see for herself what it was like; she would sneak into the webster's shop and the blacksmith's shop and see *things happening.* She was thinking about all this, and taking note of each place where a fern uncurled its lacy fronds, when the song ended and Father said something every bit as interesting as shops and schools.

He waved the letter he was holding and said, "Well, Margaret, there's a bit o' news I've been saving until matters were settled. They're settled now, and here it is."

Mum took the letter and began to read it. Martha looked up alertly. All at once Father's mysterious secret came back into her mind. Forgetting the ferns, she ran to Mum's knee.

Father's eyes were dancing. Mum scanned the letter; then she gasped and cried out happily, "Is it true, Allan?"

"Aye," said Father. "I didna tell you before lest Harry change his mind."

"That scoundrel! I had a letter from him not a fortnight gone and never a word of this did he say. It's the first time in his life my brother has kept a secret from me. Aye, but I suppose I'd better forgive him, if we're truly to be neighbors." Mum was laughing. Her blue eyes sparkled as if she were going to cry.

"Neighbors!" Martha cried out, before she remembered that children ought not to burst into grown-ups' conversations. But no one scolded. Mum beamed at her.

"Och, Martha! What do you suppose? Your uncle Harry is going to rent the South Loch farm from Father!"

"He's going to live in the valley? And Aunt Grisell and the cousins?" Martha could hardly believe her ears.

Father nodded, and Mum said, "Aye. He says he has tired of the noise and expense of the city, and he proposes to fix up the old house at South Loch. You've never been there, but your sister was born there."

Martha remembered that the house was called Fairlie and Father had visited Fairlie on his way home from Edinburgh. It was the house Father had grown up in, and Mum had lived there as a bride. She had often said that the day Father had begun work on the Stone House over here on the other side of the lake was one of the gladdest days of her life—there wasn't a draftier, smokier house than Fairlie in all of Scotland.

"Harry will have his work cut out for him, if he's to make that house fit to live in," Mum said. "But then he always did enjoy a challenge. Och, Allan, this is lovely news. Have you and Harry been cooking this up between you ever since you were in Edinburgh, then?"

Father laughed. "Something like that. I must say, I'm well pleased with the notion. My mother loved that house, and I dinna doubt it would break her heart, if she still lived, to see it falling to pieces because her son abandoned it. My father agreed that this side of the loch was a far more advantageous location, but my mother, she always said there was no dwelling in the world could match her Fairlie."

He stared off across the lake, lost in thought. Martha's mind was full of questions. She had never thought about Father's mother—she had always known her grandparents were no longer living. But now, to hear Father talking about his mother, whose heart would be broken because Father had left the old house empty, rented for so many years to a cousin who rarely troubled himself to live there . . . Martha had not thought of her grandmother as having been someone whose heart could break. She wanted to ask Father about her, but he was very quiet, looking at the lake.

"Well, she couldna ask for a nicer family to live there than my brother's," Mum said brightly. "Excepting present company, of course."

Father laughed. "Aye, it'll be grand having Harry so close. He's full of ideas for improving the house—new chimneys and glass windows and wallpaper and heaven kens what else. I must find him a good man to run the farm, though, for he kens no mair about agriculture than I do about lace knitting!"

Mum was bubbling over with ideas and plans. "We shall hire a boatman to take us across the lake for visits, and there will be parties and dances—and Alisdair and Robbie can travel with Harry's lads in the holidays. . . ." She rose, gathering up her needlework. Her linen skirts whispered around her feet.

"Come, Martha, let us tell Grisie," she said eagerly. "She'll be that glad to hear Janet and Meg are to be our neighbors. She has so longed to have girls of her age and station in the district. And there will be Rachel and Mary for you to play with, lass. Happen you can have your music lessons together; I shall have to think on it."

When Grisie heard the news, she stared openmouthed at Mum a moment, blinking. Then she actually smiled—Martha had almost forgotten that Grisie *could* smile. Grisie's face lit up, and her eyes were sparkling. She peppered Mum with questions, and both of them were talking so quickly about the things they would do when the cousins arrived that Martha had trouble keeping up. She was rather taken aback to see how suddenly Grisie's mood had changed from gloominess to joy. For just a moment Martha felt a surge of resentment— what was so wonderful about the cousins that the mere thought of their coming could make Grisie so happy?

But then the thought came to Martha that perhaps having the cousins across the lake would be enough to cure Grisie of wanting to go away. After all, Janet and Meg would be leaving their grand Edinburgh school, if they were coming to live at Fairlie.

After she had thought of it that way, Martha did not feel at all annoyed anymore. Her whole being was filled with eagerness for the cousins to hurry up and arrive.

All afternoon, Mum and Grisie and Martha talked of nothing but Fairlie and Uncle Harry's family. Neither did Cook, nor the maids, nor Duncan when he came home from school. Everyone was full of plans for the summer, for there was sure to be a steady stream of comings and goings between the Stone House and Fairlie. It was no trouble at all to boat across the lake, and from the far shore Fairlie was but a few minutes' walk. The old house was built on a rise that overlooked the lake, at the foot of the mountains that reared high above Loch Caraid's southwestern shore.

Martha could hardly eat her supper that

night, she was so excited. She remembered her cousins from the winter holidays. Rachel was exactly her age, seven. Mary was only a little girl of five. But Martha remembered liking Mary better. Rachel had been very quiet and proper; she was the sort of girl grown-ups were always saying Martha should be more like. Rachel sewed beautifully—she *liked* sewing, for heaven's sake. She could embroider all kinds of fancy stitches, even French knots.

But Mary had been fun to play with, and Martha liked the boy cousins a great deal. Mostly she had tried to stay out of the way of the two oldest girls, Janet and Meg—their endless talk of dancing and French lessons had been very dull. Martha thought Janet was the oldest, but she had never been quite clear which was which; she only remembered that one of them liked leeks and the other did not, and neither one of them could sew as well as Grisie.

There was a baby cousin, too—little Eamonn, who was still in long skirts. At least, he had been at New Year's. Martha thought of little Allan Tervish, who was just learning to walk, and how she would sometimes hold his hands and help him take his wobbly steps around his cottage. Perhaps she would be able to teach her baby cousin to walk, too.

She smiled across the supper table at Duncan, and he grinned back at her. Martha knew they were thinking the same thing. What good times they would have when Uncle Harry's family came to the valley!

The Hedger

Uncle Harry had written that he expected to arrive at Fairlie in the middle of July. All of Glencaraid was bubbling with the news. Jolly, boisterous Uncle Harry had visited many times over the years, and he was well liked by the people of the valley.

"And Lady Grisell, she's as sweet as the day is long," said Mollie to Cook and Nannie, while Martha sat listening and nibbling on a stalk of watercress. The kitchen, Martha had discovered long ago, was the best place to be if you wanted to hear what was going on in the valley.

"Me sister Helen is hopin' for a spot in the upper household," Nannie said. "She's a good lass and a hard worker. I hope Mistress Morse will put in a word for her."

"Of course she will!" said Martha, interrupting. "I'll ask her to."

"Now, Miss Martha," said Cook, "dinna ye go worriting your mither about these matters. Ye can leave the askin' to them as is involved."

It seemed to Martha that there was hardly a person on the estate who was not "involved." Everywhere she went, there was endless discussion about whom Uncle Harry and Aunt Grisell would engage as servants. They would keep old Albert on as steward, of course, and his daughter Alice as housekeeper. But Albert was getting on in years; he would need an understeward. Then there would be housemaids and kitchenmaids and dairymaids—for Fairlie was a much bigger house than the Stone House.

Father had always said the luxury of a grand

house was not worth the expense of keeping it up. He would rather put his money into improving his land. But Uncle Harry had other ideas. If Harry wanted to spend his money on maintaining a fine house and a fine table, Father said, that was fine with him.

He engaged a smart young man from Crieff to serve as Uncle Harry's overseer. Mr. Owen Banks, for that was his name, would supervise the running of the South Loch farm and collect the rents from the South Loch tenants. Martha was a little sad to hear this—it meant the South Loch farmers would no longer come to the Stone House every quarter to pay their rents and labor dues and to gather in the kitchen for storytelling and fiddle music. But there was so much else to look forward to that Martha could hardly be sorry for long.

Every day bits of news came across the lake from Fairlie—tantalizing snippets about the eleven mice that had been found nesting in one of the long-unused box beds upstairs, or the parlor chimney that no one had known was blocked up until it spit black smoke and soot all across the room. There were many rooms in the old mansion that had been closed up for a dozen years. Martha could not get her fill of hearing about Fairlie. Mum said it had a ballroom, and a dining room, and an enormous thatch-roofed kitchen that was attached to the main house by a covered passage.

"And there's a long avenue of lime trees leading up to the house, and a little terrace off the main parlor that overlooks Loch Caraid," Mum said. "Your grandfather Morse used to sit there by the hour, watching a pair of swans who lived on the loch. Loved those birds like children, he did."

"I want to see them!" Martha cried.

"Och, that was long ago, Martha. I canna say if there's any swans still there."

Martha ached to go and find out. She could not fathom how she had lived her whole life so close to this mysterious treasure of a house without ever having been taken to see it.

Mum said Martha would have plenty of time to play at Fairlie once the workmen left and the cousins arrived.

"You'll do no one any good, running about underfoot while people are working," she said. "For that matter, you've work o' your own to do, have you not? Let's have a look at your handkerchiefs."

The handkerchiefs were not the only work Martha had to do these days. Mum kept a small black book on a shelf in her room. Each of its pages was filled with row after row of words—little short words at the beginning, and great long ones in the back, long as caterpillars, with the p's and the q's pointing down like little caterpillar feet. Every day Mum gave Martha twenty new words to learn. They were only the short words now, more ant than caterpillar. Already Martha had learned dozens upon dozens of words, and still there was only the tiniest slice of book under her left hand, and a thick slab of pages left to get through under her right hand.

Some days it seemed that every word brought Fairlie back into her mind—grand, parlor, hall, chimney.

Martha did not see how she could bear the

wait. The middle of July was years away.

On a morning in June, two boys came walking up the hill from Loch Caraid. Martha saw them coming toward the Stone House, and she leaned so far out the nursery window trying to see who they were that she nearly fell out. Grisie was tying the sash of Martha's dust gown; she yanked on the ribbons and said it would have served Martha right if she'd landed on her head. Her mood had improved with the news of the cousins' impending move, but her tongue remained sharp as ever.

"You nearly ripped this sash clean off," Grisie said. "Honestly, Martha, you ought to have more sense. What does it matter who's at the door? Whoever they are, they've not come to see you."

But Grisie was wrong. Mum was calling to Martha from the bottom of the stairs: "Martha, lass! Come see what Mr. Cameron's Ian has brought!"

Martha tore out of the nursery, leaving half her sash in Grisie's hand.

The Hedger

The two boys were standing quietly in the entrance of the parlor. Martha knew them at once; they were classmates of Duncan's. One of them was named Ian, and he was the webster's youngest son. Martha had played with him and the other boy, Lewis Tucker, many a time on the Creag or at the lakeshore. Lew, whose father was the village blacksmith, was a quiet, dark-haired lad who was widely known as the only boy in school who could beat Duncan in a footrace.

Ian Cameron was as handsome as his brother Henry. He had a shock of wheat-colored hair and a lively, sunburned face. His pocket was bulging and wriggling in a most intriguing manner.

"You'd best go right into the kitchen before you take it out," Mum advised. "I dinna fancy a hedgehog loose in me parlor."

"The hedger!" Martha cried. "You've brought it!"

"Aye, miss," said Ian. "Me brother Gerald sends his respects. He says to tell ye Hedgie here would have been delivered sooner, only the courier—that's me—couldna get leave to skip school till now."

Lew grinned. "Me father had an ox chain for Mr. Tervish; that's why he let me come with Ian."

"*Someone* had to row the boat," Ian put in. "I couldna have done it, wi' this little fellow climbin' out o' me pocket every chance he gets."

Hurriedly Martha led the boys to the kitchen. Cook and Nannie were at the table chopping vegetables; they looked up inquisitively as Ian knelt on the floor by the window. Lew crouched beside him, grinning in anticipation. Martha bent over Ian, holding her breath.

Gingerly, Ian put his hand in his pocket and took out a small, spiny, brown lump. Martha saw that one end of the lump had a sharp-pointed nose, with two black-bead eyes above it. The little thing quivered and sniffed at Ian's hand.

Martha had never seen a hedgehog up close before. It was covered all over with prickly brown spines—so many spines that Martha could hardly tell where its head left off and its body began. Its face and neck were white and furry instead of spiny. The large black eyes were glistening and expressive, and fine black whiskers quivered off the sides of the funny pointed nose. It had soft brown ears, a little stub of a tail, and tiny pink feet with claws on the toes. The hedger looked up at all the faces huddled over it, and it gave a little squeak and rolled itself into a ball.

"Ouch!" said Ian, for the ball was prickly all around. "Steady on, little fellow."

"He'll soon get used to ye," said Lew. "Ian had him drinkin' milk from his finger."

"Truly?" breathed Martha.

"Aye, when Gerald first brought him home. He was just a bairn then, hardly old enough to open his eyes. Gerry, he'd spent a whole day huntin' for hedgers in the woods and the bracken. Finally spotted a female and tracked her back to her hole, and he took one o' the bairns, and here he is."

"He did that, did Gerry?" Nannie asked softly.

"Och, aye, he said he'd promised Miss Martha."

Martha could not take her eyes off the spiny ball in Ian's hand. She wanted to reach out and cuddle him in her arms, prickles and all. No wonder the poor thing was scared, she thought—he was hardly more than a bairn.

"Willna he miss his mother?" she asked. But Ian and Lew shook their heads.

"Hedgers dinna stay long wi' their mithers, like our babies do," Lew said kindly. "He'd have been out on his own by this time anyhow."

"And he likes people," Ian put in. "See, he's unrolling."

The hedgehog's nose was peeping out of the ball of spines. His tiny black claws scritch-scratched on Ian's hand. Ian set him on the floor. The hedgehog put his nose to the ground and took a few waddling steps, sniffing. Martha laughed delightedly to see his funny shuffling walk. After a while the spines on the animal's back began to lie flat instead of bristling upward. Ian said that meant he was beginning to feel at home.

"Am I to understand that ye really expect this beastie to live in me kitchen?" Cook demanded. Her stern voice did not match the interest with which she watched the hedgehog snuffle his way underneath the table.

"He's going to eat up the beetles," Martha reminded Cook. "Be a great help to you, he will."

Cook snorted. "Aye, a great help at distractin' me from me work, mair like. There, Nannie, ye've gone and let the potatoes scorch."

"What?" Nannie gasped, and ran to the pot she had left bubbling over the peats. But the potatoes were not scorched at all; it was only Cook's bit of a joke. Martha and the boys laughed, and Nannie shook her head ruefully and laughed too.

Lew and Ian told Martha to fix up a basket of leaves for the hedgehog to sleep in.

"And leave him a saucer of water to drink," Lew said.

"Or milk," Ian added. "He's right fond o' milk."

"Like our brownie," Martha said. She thought of something suddenly and cried, "Cook! Will the brownie mind having a hedger around?"

"Oho! Ye didna ask if *I* minded, I notice. Nay, ye needna trouble yourself over what Tullie will say—brownies and hedgehogs is good friends. If it were otherwise, I'd nivver have let ye bring that beastie into me kitchen, for it would nivver do to go offendin' Tullie Grayshanks!"

"That's all right, then," said Martha, much relieved. Brownies were touchy creatures. They were wonderful to have about the house as long as they were happy, for they helped with chores and brought good luck. But if he should be angered, a brownie could cause no end of mischief in a household, Martha knew, for Cook had told her many a story of curdled milk and broken dishes. Martha hoped the Stone House brownie would be pleased with his new chum. Looking at the funny little hedgehog, she did not see how Tullie could be anything but delighted.

126

The Hedger

She squatted down to watch the hedger explore his new surroundings. He nosed around under the table and, after a bit, gathered courage enough to scuttle across to the wall where the meal barrels stood. Martha crawled after him, worried that he would disappear among the peat stacks and never come out.

"Show him the larder," Ian suggested. "Once he finds himself a bit o' lunch, he'll be happy as a king."

He showed Martha how to pick up the little creature without getting pricked. Hardly daring to breathe, she cradled him in her hands. The spines tickled but did not hurt, if she was careful.

"Anyway," she said, "I'll not mind if he pricks me once in a while. I'm used to it, from sewing."

She could not believe she was holding a real live hedgehog in her own hands. The pointed nose snuffled at her fingers. The warm little body was no bigger than her hand.

"Hullo, Hedgie," she crooned at it. "You dear wee thing."

Lew said the hedgehog would keep growing, a bit. "By winter he'll be almost as big as your shoe. But he'll be wantin' his long sleep, then, and ye'll have to take him outside to a spot where there's a good lot o' leaves or brush for him to burrow in and stay warm."

"Will he come back?" Martha asked pleadingly. Now that Hedgie was here, she didn't see how she could live without him.

Ian shrugged carelessly, but Lew said in his quiet way, "I canna say. Ye nivver can tell what a wild thing will do."

"Happen he'll find himself a wife," said Ian, "and bring her back here to live."

"Och, that'd be grand!" cried Martha. "We could have a whole family o' hedgers living here."

"Whisht!" Cook cried. "One beast at a time, if ye please!"

Lew chuckled. "You needna worrit yourself, ma'am. Hedgers are no the marryin' sort. Most times they live alone. But this wee fellow seems friendly enough. Will ye keep him in the larder, then?"

The Hedger

Cook nodded. "Aye. He can have his bed there, where he'll not be under me feet. But," she added, sighing heavily as if in resignation, "we may as well leave the larder door open and give the beastie the run o' the kitchen. I've nay doubt that's how it'll end, so it may as well begin that way."

Carefully Martha carried the hedgehog into the larder, which was a sort of open closet in the back of the kitchen. The boys followed her, and Cook came behind them. The larder's walls were lined with shelves, upon which sat jar after jar of preserves—purply-red beets, pale yellow pears, golden apricot preserves like a bottle of sunshine. A meat pie that Cook had made yesterday sat upon a counter, covered with a cloth.

Martha bent down and let the hedgehog loose on the larder floor. Once again his nose went down to the ground, snuffling, and his plump body waddled across the floor. Hedgie sniffed at a basket of onions, and he sniffed at a barrel of pickled eggs. He seemed almost to know why he had been brought to the house, for he turned suddenly and went directly toward a fat black beetle that was scuttling across the floor. The hedgehog scurried to the beetle and, quick as a wink, snapped it up, while Martha and the boys cheered him on.

"Here," said Cook gruffly, taking an empty straw basket off a high shelf. "Ye can have this for his bed. He's got to earn his keep, mind," she added. She was so gruff that Martha knew she liked the hedgehog very much and didn't want to admit it.

The basket was inspected by both boys and pronounced perfectly suited for the job. It was a wide-mouthed, shallow basket that Cook herself had woven, and when it had been filled with leaves and pine needles from the wood behind the garden, it seemed like a hedgehog's idea of a castle. Martha helped Hedgie climb into the box and watched him burrow under the leaves as if he were snuggling up beneath a nice woolen blanket. He turned himself around and laid down his head and promptly went to sleep, with his prickles poking up through the leaves and his little pointed nose peeping out.

"Look at him, the lazy wee beast!" Cook cried. "Makes himself right at home, he does."

"Hedgers like best to sleep during the day," Ian explained. "He'll wake up in the evening and be ready to hunt."

Lew nodded. "Or if ye wish to play wi' him, ye can wake him up gentle like and give him a bit o' milk. He'll make friends wi' ye fast."

Lew was right. After the boys left, Martha couldn't help but go back and pick Hedgie up again out of his leafy nest. He woke up the tiniest bit and blinked his glistening black eyes at her, then put his head down on her hand and went back to sleep. Martha hardly dared to breathe, sitting there on the larder floor with the warm body slumbering in her hands. It was as though Hedgie knew her already and felt safe with her. Martha's heart filled up and felt like it would burst.

After that, Martha could not get out of bed fast enough in the mornings. She would run downstairs in her nightgown to greet Hedgie and fill his dish of water and make sure his box of leaves was fresh and neat. Every night she set out a saucer of milk for him, just as Cook set out bannocks and cream for the brownie. Sometimes Cook let Martha feed Hedgie a bit of cheese, and when she squatted down on the floor and held out the cheese, he came waddling right over to her and pushed gently at her fingers with his nose. Martha thought there could be nothing in the world more wonderful than having a real live hedgehog who knew you so well that his spines lay comfortably flat when you picked him up.

And Cook was happy, because the beetles were kept out of her bread.

Jam

In July the thrilling news came sailing across the lake: The cousins had arrived at Fairlie! The girl cousins, at least. Uncle Harry's boys were still at the academy in Edinburgh with Robbie and Alisdair. But Janet and Meg and Rachel and Mary—and the baby, of course—were all at the old mansion with their mother and father.

It was quickly arranged that Mum and Grisie would go to Fairlie to help Aunt Grisell get settled in, and Rachel and Mary would be brought to the Stone House to keep them out from underfoot. They had no governess yet; their last governess had not wanted to leave Edinburgh for such a remote post. Mum said the three little girls would be quite all right with Mollie to see that they did not get into too much mischief.

Martha didn't quite like the idea of Grisie getting to see Fairlie before she herself did. But she knew it would be selfish to say so, so she didn't let Mum see that she minded. Anyway, it was fun to think of having the run of the house with Mary and Rachel.

She was cheerful about the arrangement until the moment came for Mum to kiss her good-bye and get into the ferryman's boat to cross the lake. Then Martha realized that there was another side to the plan that she had not thought about yet. She would not see Mum for a week at least. A whole week!

Grisie was watching from the her seat in the ferryboat. Martha blinked fiercely and did not cry. *I will not cry,* she told herself. *I will not—not with Grisie watching.*

Mum squeezed Martha tight and let her go,

134

and then she stepped into the boat and settled herself on the seat beside Grisie. Sandy climbed in after her. He was going along to carry Mum and Grisie's baggage to Fairlie once they reached the other side of the lake.

Mum waved merrily; the ferryman put his oars into the water and shoved off. The boat slipped away from the shore, and the blue arms of the water tugged it toward the center of the lake. Martha watched it grow smaller and smaller.

Martha made herself cheer, so Grisie wouldn't know how badly she wanted to cry. She cheered and halloed with all her might; she was determined that Mum and Grisie would hear her all the way across the lake. But as soon as the boat had slipped out of sight, she turned and raced with stinging eyes up the hill and into the house.

Cook called Martha into the kitchen. She and Nannie, with their sleeves rolled up and their oldest aprons on, were just beginning the sticky business of making blackberry jam. Cook took one look at Martha's face and disappeared to her alcove at the back of the kitchen. She came out brandishing an apron even more ancient and stained than the one that she herself was wearing. She swathed Martha in the apron and tucked her red curls beneath a spare linen cap of Nannie's, a ruffled white one with a broad red ribbon tied around it.

Martha ran to the look in the looking glass in the parlor; she had to laugh to see herself looking so exactly like a kitchen servant. A quarter of an hour later, her lips stained purple from blackberry juice and the old apron proudly exhibiting a new assortment of stains, Martha had forgotten all about the terrible feeling of watching Mum grow smaller and smaller upon the water. Cook let her help pick over the berries and teased that the new scullery maid ate a great deal faster than she worked.

"Happen so," said Nannie, "but she works with a right good will, and ye canna ask better than that."

"These berries are lovely," Martha said,

with her mouth puckered full. "Did you pick them yesterday? I wish you'd taken me with you."

"Och, ye were busy at your lessons," said Nannie. "Like the good lass ye are. But dinna ye fret—I missed out on the fun o' it same as ye. Cook and me was polishing silver all the day long, dinna ye mind it? Me brother Paul had the pickin' o' the berries, and me wee sisters. Me mither sent them out with pails just to keep them busy while she was after makin' soap, and didna they come back with all their pails full and their caps and aprons too!"

Martha wanted to know exactly where the children had gone, and how many pails they had filled.

"Do you think there are any berries left on the bushes? I could take my cousins, when they get here."

But Cook clucked her tongue and said she doubted Rachel and Mary could make the walk.

"Three miles off and halfway up Ben Fallon,

it is," she said, "to the spot where the best blackberries grow. Your cousins be city lasses, Martha; they're no used to traipsin' about the hills." She lifted the heavy kettle full of berries and sugar, and she hung it from the iron crane in the fireplace. "The bushes in the garden ought to come ripe in another day or so. Ye and your cousins can have the pickin' o' them then."

"Aye, we'll do that," said Martha. But it would not be the same as picking the wild bushes up on the shoulder of Ben Fallon, the mountain where the clean wind sailed through stands of silvery birch and whisked above carpets of bluebell.

The berries bubbled over the fire, and Nannie and Cook set to work readying the rows of glass jars for filling when the jam was ready to pour. Mollie came in, her thin cheeks flushed and her clothes covered with dust, and said she had finished all the upstairs work.

"If there's a cleaner floor in all the county than the master and mistress's, I'd just like to see it," she said triumphantly. "Been waitin',

I have, for a day when everyone was out o' the house. Martha, ye stay out o' there this afternoon, mind. I want it lookin' fine for your father when he comes back from looking at his trees."

"That's all right, I'm making jam," Martha said. "I'll not have time for playing upstairs today."

"*She's* makin' jam, says Herself," Cook snorted. "And Nannie and me is fine ladies sippin' tea with our little fingers prinked, I guess."

Mollie grinned. "In that case," she said, putting on a haughty accent, "do pour me a cup, Lady Margery Anne." She made a little mocking bow to Cook, who solemnly curtseyed back, delicately lifting her berry-streaked apron between her fingertips as though it were a silken skirt.

Martha howled with laughter. "Margery Anne!" she cried.

"And what's funny about that?" Cook demanded. "I'll no argue with ye for laughin' at the 'Lady' part. But there's naught so

amusin' about callin' me 'Margery Anne'—
that bein' me given name, as it is."

"What?" Martha nearly choked. She stared
at Cook, dumbstruck. Nannie and Mollie giggled across the table.

Cook was trying very hard to look offended,
but she could not help chuckling at the sight
of Martha's astonished face. "Ye didna think
me mither named her bairn 'Cook,' did ye?
Margery Anne I was, on the day o' me chris-
tenin', and Margery Anne I am today. Now—
are ye goin' to stir that jam, or do ye intend
to spend your afternoon scrapin' it off the bottom o' the kettle?"

Martha jumped up and grabbed the spoon.
"Och, I'll stir it—Margery Anne."

"We'll have none o' your sauce, lass," said
Cook. "'Cook' will do just fine from ye."

All that afternoon, the kitchen was hot and
crowded and merry. Martha was amazed when
Cook said it was nearly suppertime.

"But Duncan's not home from school yet,"
she said, and then she remembered that Duncan
was not coming home tonight, nor indeed any

night this week. Mum had decided that he might as well go back and forth to school from Fairlie, as it was closer to the village than the Stone House. The lump that had been there when Mum left came back into Martha's throat. But then Father came in from the fir wood, and Martha ran and pulled him into the kitchen and showed him all the jam she had helped to make. Father laughed and told Cook she had the patience of a saint. Martha thought that was very odd, because Cook did not seem to her at all a patient sort of person.

As a treat, Father let Martha have her supper in the kitchen with Cook and the maids. It felt like a party, sitting next to Cook on a bench in back of the kitchen, where the cool evening breeze blew in from the garden. Hedgie played on the floor at her feet, pouncing on the tidbits of bread and cheese Martha tossed down to him.

It had been such a busy day that when bedtime came, Martha was too tired to think about sleeping alone for the first time in her life. Mollie tucked her in and sat beside her for a while, singing, with the box bed's door-panel open.

"Oh, can ye sew cushions, and can ye sew
     sheets?
And can ye sing bal-la-loo when the bairnie
     greets?
And hush-a-ba, birdie, and hush-a-ba, lamb,
And hush-a-ba, birdie, my bonnie wee lamb."

Martha stretched like a cat, her arms and legs reaching out to feel the cool sheets. Sleepily, she thought how strange it was to move your legs as far as they could go, and not bump into other legs that kicked you back to your own side. She heard Mollie singing softly:

"Now hush-a-ba lambie, and hush-a-ba dear,
Now hush-a-ba lambie, thy minnie is here.
The wild wind is ravin', thy minnie's heart's
     sair,
The wild wind is ravin', but dinna ye care."

and then it was morning.

Cousins

It was strange, waking up alone in the nursery. Strange enough not to have Grisie in bed beside her—but beyond strange, almost terrible, not to hear the door-panel of Duncan's bed slam open, followed by the slap of his feet hitting the floor.

That morning Martha had a whole bowl of porridge and a jug of cream all to herself. She had never in her life had a bowl and jug that need not be shared with anybody. But there was no joy in being mistress of the porridge. Martha thought of Duncan eating his breakfast in the beautiful Fairlie dining room, with Mum and Grisie and jolly Uncle Harry and the others. She wished Rachel and Mary would hurry up and get to the Stone House. It hurt to think of everyone else having a wonderful time together in the grand house on the other side of the lake.

Mollie came in to brush Martha's hair, since Grisie was not there to do it.

"I dinna see why I couldna go to Fairlie too," Martha said, wincing under Mollie's brisk strokes. Mollie was more cheerful than Grisie in the morning, but she didn't have Grisie's gentle way with the hairbrush. "I'll be the last one to see it. It's hardly fair that I've lived my whole life right across the loch from it and no one ever took me to see it before."

"Ye'll see the house soon enough," Mollie said comfortingly. "It's stood for a hundred years and mair; I'm thinkin' it'll not tumble down before ye get a chance to visit."

"But I'll be the last one," Martha repeated. That was not really what was bothering her, but she did not know how else to talk about the troublesome feelings that came when she thought about everyone enjoying themselves at Fairlie, the grand and splendid house. She was half afraid that Mum would decide to live there forever, or that Duncan would never come home. It would be so much simpler for him to live on the same side of the lake as the school.

"Ouch, Mollie, dinna yank so!" she cried out, and the crossness in her voice made Mollie murmur, "Mercy, lass! Calm yourself; I'm nearly finished."

But her quick hands went on whisking the brush through Martha's tangled curls, until Martha's scalp stung so much that she couldn't think about wonderful Fairlie anymore.

Sandy had spent the night on the other side of the lake. He came back to the Stone House not long after breakfast, with the cousins, Rachel and Mary.

Martha ran shouting out the door to greet them. They hung back shyly, staring at her with wide-opened eyes. Rachel had long, thin, pale hair tucked neatly beneath a straw bonnet trimmed with silk flowers. Her dress was very white. She did not wear a dust-gown—neither did Mary, and Mary was only five!

Martha fell silent herself, eyeing her cousins warily. They looked like flowers in their crisp, shining white dresses and rose-sprinkled hats. Rachel wore a pink sash and Mary a blue one.

Martha could not remember having noticed their clothes last winter, when they had visited. But then, she had not paid them much notice except at night when they were crowded into the box bed together. The boy cousins, Rachel and Mary's brothers, had been more fun to play with.

"Ah, here's our visitors," said Mollie cheerfully, coming outside in her apron and cap. "Miss Rachel, Miss Mary. Mercy, how ye've grown since last ye were here! Martha, did ye kiss yer cousins?"

Awkwardly Martha kissed each of them hello. She wanted to take them to see Hedgie first thing, but Cook was cutting up fish from the lake for drying this morning and must not be disturbed until she was finished.

So Martha said, "Mum said I might show you the Creag, and the flax field, and the barns, and everywhere. It was too cold at Hogmanay."

But Mollie bit her lip and said the cousins' frocks were too fine to spoil with romping.

"Bide a wee until I unpack their things," she said, reaching for the baggage Sandy had carried up from the ferryboat. "I expect ye've brought some play clothes?" she asked Rachel kindly, and Rachel nodded. Mollie said she would see to the unpacking just as soon as she finished the downstairs dusting, and she sent the children up to the nursery to play until dinner.

Martha stared listlessly around the nursery; never had it seemed so dull a place. The hearth, the beds, some chests against the walls. She was not sure what to do with the cousins. Rachel stood like a statue, staring around the room.

But Mary ran to Martha's box bed and said, "That's where we slept before! I want to go in."

She had pulled off her hat and was sliding the bed's door-panel open when Rachel hissed at her to be still.

"Mind your manners," Rachel whispered. "You mustna take off your hat till you're asked. Nor climb on the furniture," she added darkly.

Martha cried out in disbelief.

"Are you waiting for *me* to tell you to take your hat off? Dinna be a goose, Rachel, I'm no your mother."

Right away she regretted her words, for Rachel's eyes filled with tears.

"Och, I—I didna mean—" Martha stammered. "You're no *really* a goose. I only meant . . ."

She didn't know what to say. She was afraid to say anything, if Rachel was going to cry just because Martha said "goose." If Rachel expected Martha to behave like a grown-up lady, and say "Please might I take your bonnets" and "Do make yourselves at home"— what could you do with a girl like that!

She tried to think what Mum would do to

entertain guests. Grown-ups talked mostly about the weather, as far as she could remember, and each other's health.

"You are both looking well," she said stiffly.

Rachel nodded gravely. Mary giggled and said, "We are well, only Rachel didna want to come. She hates to leave Mother."

Rachel looked daggers at Mary. But Martha was so relieved, she laughed out loud and said, "Is that true, Rachel? I ken just how you feel! But dinna fret—we shall have heaps o' fun— I ken we will, with no one to look after us. Mollie willna be a bother. And Cook will make us all kinds of nice things to eat. I dinna expect we'll see much o' Father. He's out about the estate, mostly, except mealtimes."

Rachel gave her a thin smile. She still stood uncertainly in the middle of the room, so Martha said, "Here, take off your bonnet. What shall we play?" A thought popped into her head and she cried, "Och, I ken! Let's play that this room is the Stone House, and Mum and Father's room is Fairlie! You can live there, and I'll visit in my carriage."

Mary clapped her hands. Even Rachel's eyes lit up, for it was a very good plan.

"That's the name of our new house, Mary," she said.

Mary rolled her eyes and said of course she knew that; *she* wasn't a goose. Martha began to think she liked Mary quite a lot, even if she was only a little thing of five years old.

"All right, then," Martha said. "Mum and Father's bed shall be the main part of the house. The fireplace must be the kitchen, and the round rug by Father's chair shall be the terrace where we watch the swans."

"There aren't any swans," said Rachel. "Our steward says there used to be, but that was ages ago."

"Oh," said Martha. She had forgotten, for a moment, that Rachel and Mary had already seen Fairlie and indeed knew more about it than she did. Mum had said the swans might be gone from that side of the lake, but somehow hearing it from Rachel was worse.

"What about the great hall?" Mary was asking. "With the painted ceiling?"

Martha shook back her hair. She must not let Rachel see that she was upset about some silly old swans.

"The great hall will be under the bed," she told Mary firmly. "That's the downstairs."

When all the important details were set, Rachel and Mary went to Mum and Father's room.

Martha climbed into a make-believe carriage and cracked a make-believe whip over the heads of invisible horses. As long as she was having a carriage ride, she might as well be the driver. Bumping behind the horses, she rode at a brisk pace out of the nursery, past the stone staircase that led to the lower floor, and into the big bedroom that belonged to her mother and father.

Their large canopied bed stood off to one side, hung all around with chintz curtains. The airy cotton fabric was printed with a cheerful pattern of red poppies, so that the bed was like a summer meadow. On the other side of the room was the dinner table, and in a corner was Father's writing desk. Around the wide

stone hearth were several stools and chairs, where the family sat in the evenings eating apples and listening to the fairy stories Mum liked to tell while she was spinning.

But the spinning wheel stood silently in a corner today. Martha felt a sudden throbbing in her chest. Mum would not be there to spin tonight, or tell stories, or tuck Martha into bed with a kiss.

Martha swallowed fiercely. She was no baby to cry over little things. Rachel was going to be away from her mother too. Tossing her head, Martha galloped up to the flowery bed and halted the carriage with a flourish.

A bedpost had been designated the front door. Martha knocked boldly.

"Mercy," she declared, "what a fine coat of arms!"

For Father had told her that the MacNab family arms were emblazoned over the door, three crescents and a boat. Father's mother had been a daughter of the MacNab clan, one of the oldest families in Scotland. Glencaraid had belonged to her father, Martha's great-grandfather, who was a descendant of the first MacNab ever to settle in this part of the Highlands. It made Martha feel proud to think of the long line of her ancestors stretching back to the olden days when Scotland was a land of chieftains and warriors.

Mary's head appeared between the poppy-strewn folds of a bed-curtain. "I'm the steward," she whispered loudly, "and I must come down the winding stair."

She trotted down the three short steps of the little wooden stepstool that Mum used to climb into the high, curtained bed. Solemnly she ushered Martha inside the house. On hands and knees, with heads ducked almost to the floor, they crawled under the great bed. The feathers in the mattress above them made a rustling sound whenever Rachel moved.

"Here's the great hall," Mary said, presenting the bare floorboards with a sweep of her hand.

Martha brushed a spider off her skirt and spoke admiringly of the furniture and the lovely view from the windows.

"Aren't you coming up?" asked Rachel plaintively.

So Martha and Mary climbed out from under the bed. Rachel was waiting for them in the "parlor," among the fat feather pillows at the head of the bed. The curtains hung closely around the four sides of the bed, and overhead there bloomed a canopy of the same scarlet-poppy cloth. The four oaken bedposts rose as tall and sturdy as trees, or the masts of a ship. The bed, laid with a leaf-green coverlet, seemed vast and cozy at the same time.

Mary stood up and jumped on the bed. She lifted up her feet so that she fell with a *plop* right on her bottom, sinking deep into the soft feather tick. Martha thought it looked like great fun and was going to stand up and try it herself, but Rachel broke out scolding, "Mary! In your shoes and everything! You mustna!"

"Och, leave me be," Mary grumbled. But Rachel fussed at her until Mary promised to behave.

"You must be my daughter," Rachel said

earnestly, "for I'm the lady of the house. That's the proper way to play."

Martha thought Mary's play would have been more fun. But it was great fun, none-theless, to pretend to take tea and cakes in the grand Fairlie parlor, and to admire the pic-tures on the walls and the view of the lake. The last few weeks, Father and Mum and Grisie had talked about Fairlie so much that Martha could see in her mind exactly what it looked like, for all she had never been there.

Mostly they had talked about dull things like wallpaper and closets. But there had been funny stories now and then about things that had happened when Mum and Father had lived in the house, long before Martha was born. Even better were the stories that came from the days when Father had been a little boy growing up at Fairlie. Once, Father had said, a mouse had fallen off the rafters of the kitchen ceiling and landed right in a tureen of soup.

"Ugh!" Rachel shuddered when Martha told the story.

"Did he eat it?" Mary asked, her voice low with horror.

"Nay, of course not," Martha laughed. "But it did get served at table. The cook heard a splash but never saw what it was. The maid was serving Father his soup when suddenly she gave a scream, and there was the mouse, floating in Father's bowl!"

Rachel cried out in digust.

"Och, the poor wee mouse," said Mary.

"Of course they threw the soup on the rubbish heap," Martha said. "But Father said his great-aunt Harriet thought it was a frightful waste—she said it was a sin and a shame, and it wouldna have hurt Father to fish out the mouse and eat the soup!"

"She never!" said Rachel.

"She did. But my grandmother said her son was neither hawk nor hound, and she'd not have him eat any mouse broth. 'Nor the rest of us neither,' she said, and she told the maid to go around the table and empty everyone's bowl back into the tureen. Father said they had bread and cheese for dinner that day, and not a soul complained but Aunt Harriet!"

"That was good of the grandmother," said Mary. "I like her."

"Me too," said Martha. "I'd have done the same thing. I'd never make anyone eat something so revolting."

"But it *is* wicked to be wasteful," Rachel said doubtfully. She chewed on her hair ribbon, thinking. "I think it would be all right not to eat the bowl of soup you found the mouse in. But they oughtn't to have thrown away the rest of it."

Martha sighed. Inside her was a tiny wish that Rachel had stayed at Fairlie with Aunt Grisell and the others.

After a while Mollie came and shooed them out of Mum's bedroom. "I've me dustin' and sweepin' to do," she said. "And a bed to make, it seems," she added wryly, surveying the rumpled bedcovers that had served as Fairlie's ballroom floor.

"Is Cook finished with the fish?" Martha asked, and Mollie said she was.

So Martha cried, "Come, let's go and see if Hedgie's awake!"

The kitchen held the pungent odor of fish. Cook stood at the long table, peeling turnips and humming to herself in a rather fierce manner. Her large round face was red from the heat of the July afternoon. Rachel and Mary stood shyly in the kitchen doorway, watching Cook's plump hands make short work of the turnip skins with her sharp knife.

"Neeps!" Martha cried in delight, and hurried to the table for a piece of turnip. Cook flipped Martha a little slice with the tip of her knife.

"Well, Miss Rachel, is it?" said Cook. "And Miss Mary. Ye've grown, both o' ye."

Rachel bobbed uncertainly, as if she didn't know whether she ought to curtsey or not. Cook smiled at her and offered Rachel and Mary each a piece of turnip.

"And one for Hedgie, please," Martha begged.

"Ye'd think he was a human bairn, the way ye cosset him," said Cook, but she gave Martha a bit of turnip for the hedgehog. Martha led the cousins into the larder and showed them the wooden box. It was filled now with sweet-smelling hay that Sandy had brought in from the barns. Hedgie was sleeping, but Martha took him out and gave him the turnip, and he sat in her hands and nibbled at it until it was all gone. Rachel and Mary's eyes were wide with awe. Neither of them wanted to hold Hedgie, but they could not get enough of look-ing at him.

Then Cook told them to be good lasses and go wash up for dinner. A kettle of her good lamb broth was simmering on the hearth, thick with barley and vegetables. "Be quick!" she said. "Ye'll no want to keep his lairdship waitin'."

That, Martha agreed, was certainly true. Father was very stern about being prompt for meals. She set Hedgie back in his box, where his plump little body made a dent in the hay. Mary did not want to leave the larder; Martha had to take her by the hand and lead her up the stairs. Rachel came anxiously behind, chewing on the end of her hair ribbon.

When Martha slipped into her seat at the table in Mum and Father's room, her stomach turned over suddenly. It was strange to see Mum's seat empty. Rachel was sitting in Grisie's seat, and Mollie had put Mary's bowl across from Martha, at Duncan's chair.

Father came in and gave a cordial greeting to the cousins. Rachel looked stricken and tried unsuccessfully to curtsey from her chair. Father didn't notice, but Martha did.

Father took his seat and said grace. Mollie poured him a mug of ale and ladled soup into everyone's bowl. Father ate silently in his carved chair at the head of the table. He was wearing the white wig that made him look so solemn and stern, and he did not speak. Mum was usually the one who kept conversations rolling at meals. Father had a way of sinking deep into his thoughts. He was like that now, taking spoonfuls of broth without seeming to see the bowl.

Martha watched him and wondered if he had forgotten there was anyone else at the table. He seemed a great distance away. She had never been alone with Father at dinner before.

A lump came into Martha's throat. Every bit of her was missing Mum.

She spooned up a piece of lamb, tender and savory. As she chewed she thought suddenly of the mouse Father had found in his bowl when he was little. Perhaps—the thought nearly made her choke—perhaps he had been just her age. How he must have shouted when he discovered the poor mouse! She tried to imagine him a little boy, poking at the drowned mouse with his spoon. All she could see was an image of Duncan in a white wig and tail-coat. It made her giggle, and the sound was loud as the peal of a bell in the quiet room.

Father looked her way, eyebrows raised.

"Beg pardon," she gasped. She felt Rachel's shocked stare. Rachel would never laugh at the table. But Mary was looking as though she might burst out giggling herself.

Father didn't say anything. He had already looked away, lost in his own thoughts again.

They were important thoughts, Martha knew, for being laird of an estate—even a smallish one like Glencaraid—meant a terrible lot of worry. She wished Father would think them out loud; she would like to know. They had to do with tree plantations most likely, and the flax crop and the oats and barley, and the herds of black cattle up in the high meadows, and whether any of the cottagers would pay his rent in coin money this quarter instead of in rabbits and hens and honey. Those were the kinds of things Father talked to Mum about, during ordinary dinners.

Martha found herself gulping her broth as fast as she could. She wished she could go to the kitchen and eat with Cook and the maids, as she had done last night. She wished she could fly across the lake to Mum, right this minute. It would be fun to turn into a bird and perch outside the windows at Fairlie, peeking in at Mum and Grisie and Duncan.

That made her remember the story Auld Mary had told at the waulking, and what the kirk mice had said about fern seeds. Martha had been so caught up in thinking about the cousins moving to Fairlie that she had nearly forgotten her plans to harvest the seeds that could make a person invisible. Now she remembered, and at once an idea came into her head. She would use the magic of the seeds to turn herself invisible, and then she would sneak into a boat and cross the lake and see her mother without having to wait for the whole long week to be over. It was such a lovely notion that Martha came close to laughing out loud again, just from the satisfaction of having thought of it.

The Best-Laid Schemes

After that first day, Father told the servants they needn't bother with serving formal meals; the little girls could take their meals in the nursery, he said. He was very busy and distracted, and he grumbled more than Martha had ever heard him grumble in his life. Nothing seemed to behave as he wanted it to, or to be where he thought it should be. He couldn't find a decent goose feather to use for a pen, and he had to make do with crow quills. Crow feathers made dull, scratchy, coarse pens, and Father hated to use them. He grumbled about his wig (he couldn't get it brushed properly) and his tea (he couldn't seem to pour in the right amount of milk).

It gave Martha the strangest feeling to realize that Father was missing Mum as much as she was.

The three girls felt without saying so that it was best to keep out of Father's way. If it had been up to Rachel, they would have stayed tucked in the nursery all the day long, sewing, knitting, studying their lessons.

But it was not up to Rachel. Martha didn't see how anyone could think of staying inside all day, when outdoors there was the lovely green-and-golden summer all around. She took Rachel and Mary out to nibble mint sprigs in the garden and to sail leaf boats in the lake. She half led, half pulled them up to the top of the Creag, where the old stone wall stood proudly against the sweeping expanse of sky.

She showed the cousins how to paint battle stripes on their faces like the ancient Pict warriors her brother Alisdair had told her about. Berry juice mixed with dirt made a good, thick paint. With its garish red-brown markings, even timid Rachel's face looked, if not exactly warlike, then respectably wild. But though Rachel gave in to being painted, she could not be convinced to play Picts and Scots. While Martha and Mary ran shrieking down the hill, Rachel hung back nervously, chewing her hair ribbons until they were fringed at the ends.

Each day, Martha outdid herself in thinking up exciting new games to play with Mary and Rachel. Upturned chairs in the nursery made fine, high-spirited horses; Mollie and Nannie's attic room was a dim cave perfect for outlaws to hide in. The girls pored over Martha's *Dick Whittington*, and they all took turns playing the pianoforte until Cook came into the parlor scolding and waving her wooden spoon in the air.

Another day, Martha took out her fairy dolls and announced that they were going to move to the big city. After looking over and rejecting several possible residences, including the nursery cabinet and the top stair, the dolls decided upon a splendid apartment on a shelf in Mum's spice cupboard, beautifully furnished with glass-stoppered bottles and smelling deliciously of cinnamon. Duncan's tin soldiers were borrowed to provide upstairs neighbors for the fairies, and Martha collected an assortment of buttons and thimbles to serve as their dishes. Rachel proved to have an excellent sense of style when it came to decorating the dolls' living quarters. The three girls found that an afternoon passed in the blink of an eye when they were all squeezed into the closet staging domestic adventures for the dolls.

And all the time Martha was thinking about how best to bring off her plan of collecting the magic fern seeds. The mice in Auld Mary's tale had said the seeds must be harvested at midnight. That would be tricky, Martha knew—especially since she' shared her bed with Rachel and Mary. She did not think it likely she could slip out of bed in the night without waking them up.

At last she decided the best thing to do was

to include them in the plan. They could sneak out with her, and they would all turn invisible together. After all, Rachel and Mary were missing their mother too. They would probably like to slip across the lake to have a glimpse of her.

Even so, Martha knew it would not be easy to convince Rachel to go outside in the middle of the night, since Rachel was so timid and nervous. Mary would go along with anything her sister did, so it was just a matter of getting Rachel to agree.

Martha decided to wait until they were all in bed. The rest of that day she could not think of anything else, but she managed to keep quiet about the plan until nighttime, after they had all said good night to Father and been tucked into the box bed by Mollie.

Then she whispered, "Rachel, you mustna go to sleep tonight. Stay awake, do you hear?"

"What?" Rachel murmured, sounding half asleep already. Mary's breathing was heavy and slow on Martha's other side.

"You must stay awake," Martha repeated.

"We'll wake Mary when it's time."

Rachel's voice was cross. "Time for what? I don't know what you're talking about, Martha."

So Martha whispered the whole plan— slipping outside, gathering the fern seeds, what they would do with them once they had them.

Rachel stopped sounding cross and sounded frightened instead. "But if we're caught—your father . . ."

Martha brushed her worries aside. "We willna get caught. We'll wait till everyone is sleeping, and we'll be outside just a moment. I ken just where to go. There are ferns grow-ing not three steps from the front door; you needna be afraid. We'll get the seeds tonight, and tomorrow after breakfast we can go and see our mothers."

Rachel made a wistful sound, and Martha knew her cousin was enticed by the prospect of seeing her mother. But it took a great deal more arguing to finally convince her. Mary woke up in the process, and when Rachel saw how readily Mary agreed to the plan, she reluctantly gave in.

"I'm only going along to look after Mary," she said, with rather more fire than Martha had ever heard from her. "Mother said I was to take good care of her and not let her get into mischief." She added despairingly, "I think this *is* mischief, Martha. Hadn't we better not do it?"

"Mischief," answered Martha promptly, having given some thought to this subject before, "is only things that might hurt someone else, or inconvenience them. We shan't make a speck o' trouble for anybody."

After so much discussion, all three girls felt quite wide awake. Now they grew quiet and listened; through the walls of the box bed they could hear faint, muffled noises of Father moving about in his bedroom, and attic floorboards creaking under Mollie's feet.

"That's good," Martha whispered. "It's very late already, if Mollie has gone upstairs."

They listened awhile longer. Father's room was silent. Every few minutes Martha would ask the others if they were still awake, and Rachel, exasperated, would say huffily that yes, they were, and would she please stop asking.

At last the only sounds they could hear were their own. Above them, the floorboards had stopped creaking.

Quietly Martha slid open the box bed's wooden door-panel. She could not hear anything except her own heart thumping.

"Still, we'd better wait a bit," she told the others. "I'm not quite certain—I dinna suppose it's *quite* midnight yet."

The nursery was not as dark as the closed box bed had been. In summer the sun lingered low in the sky almost the whole night long. The room glowed with a pale dusky light that crept in through the cracks of the shutters.

Martha dangled her legs over the side of the bed. She had expected the room to be pitch dark, and somehow it was scarier to see the dim outlines of things than not to be able to see anything at all. Her brothers' empty beds were dark, looming shapes across the room.

The Best-Laid Schemes

Behind Martha, Mary fidgeted restlessly. Slowly Martha slid to the floor. "It must be close to midnight now," she said. "Wait here until I tell you to come."

She crept to the nursery door, sliding a hand along the wall of the box bed to help her keep her way. She could see a little more now. Wall and furniture were different shades of dark.

There was no light coming from Father's room, and no noise from downstairs apart from some creaks and rustles that were only house sounds. Martha felt sure that they were midnight sounds: The air was very still. She began to worry that they would be too late harvesting the seeds and the magic wouldn't work.

As quickly as she dared, she slipped back into the nursery and helped her cousins climb out of bed. Their white nightgowns glowed pale as ghosts.

"Dinna say a word," she warned them. Silently they tiptoed out of the nursery, along the hall, down the stairs. The stairs were colder than the floorboards. In winter they would have been cold as ice, but now, in summer, they felt pleasantly cool on Martha's feet.

They all came safely to the bottom of the stairs and crept across the hall to the great front door. The key was in the lock; Martha had to use two hands to turn it, but after that it was easy to open the door. Sandy kept its hinges so well oiled that it made hardly any noise as it swung open.

The cool night air blew in on the girls. Frogs called to each other among the reeds at the shore. As Martha stepped out of the house, a sudden wild longing leaped up in her heart. She wanted to run to the Creag and see how the whole valley looked at night—she wanted to go down to the lake and see if perhaps the water fairy Mum had told her about was out gathering the spills of moonlight that lay shimmering upon the dark water. There was a mushroom ring near the waulking place, beyond the old pine tree; Mum said the fairies held dances there on still, moonlit nights. Martha burned to see them. She would go explore—she *would!*

But Rachel was still standing in the doorway;

Martha could tell that her cousin was too afraid to step outside the house. Rachel would never agree to running around the farm in the dark. Anyway, the fern seeds were waiting—suppose it was past midnight already?

Martha darted to the clump of ferns that grew not far from the Stone House door, beside Mum's heather bench. "Here they are," she whispered to her cousins. Mary had squeezed past Rachel and come outside, and she stood leaning on the heather bench while Martha crouched beside the ferns.

Martha turned over the leaves to look at the undersides, but she could not see the seeds in the dark. Eagerly she scraped her fingers along the leaves and tried to knock the spores loose into her palm. All the while Rachel was making nervous noises in the doorway, and Mary was saying "Have you got them? Have you got them?" in a whisper that was somehow louder than her ordinary voice.

At last Martha felt certain she had some of the seeds in her hand. She and Mary crept back through the doorway, where Rachel stood anxiously waiting. Quietly Martha pushed the door closed. Then, huddled in the hallway, they all ate the seeds, or at any rate they tried to. The seeds were so small, and the hall so dark, that it was difficult to tell if any of the tiny black specks actually made it into their mouths. Martha found herself swallowing and swallowing and having no idea whether the seeds had indeed gone down. They might still be stuck to her tongue, for all she could tell.

"I don't think it worked," Rachel said doubtfully. "I can still see you."

"Of course, because we're all invisible together," It was only a guess, but as soon as Martha had said it, she felt certain it must be the case.

Suddenly all kinds of questions came to mind that she had not considered before: How long would the being invisible last? What would happen tomorrow when Mollie could not find them in their beds? Wouldn't Father be terribly worried when he learned the girls were missing? How could they think of going off to see their mothers and enjoy themselves, when Father and Cook and everyone would be so upset because the little girls could not be found?

There was no time to think of answers. A noise in the kitchen—noises—footsteps. Rachel and Mary froze. For a second Martha thought it was going to be the brownie; she would see him at last!

But it was not. It was a heavy tread that Martha knew well: It was Cook. She was coming through the kitchen and would be in the hall at any moment.

"Dinna say a word!" Martha hissed to her cousins. "She canna see us, mind. We're invisible."

Cook's footsteps paused; there was a dreadful moment of silence; then they started again and Cook came shuffling out of the kitchen in a white nightgown and cap, with an iron frying pan in her hand. The girls stood like statues, watching Cook walk toward them. Martha had never seen Cook in anything but her daytime clothes. The long nightgown billowed around Cook's ankles; a braid of gray hair hung over her shoulder. Martha almost laughed aloud, not so much because Cook looked funny (though she did, with the girlish braid hanging daintily below the old-fashioned ruffle of her cap) as because it was so frightening to have Cook walking right toward her, looking right at her, almost as if she could see Martha.

She canna see me, Martha reminded herself, and she felt better. Still, she was half afraid Cook would hear her heart thumping. She was afraid Mary would squeak or Rachel would cry and they would all be caught. She wondered how she could ever have thought of doing something so naughty as creeping out of the house in the middle of the night. Until now it had only seemed a little naughty, in the way that begging for cookies was just a little naughty.

Now, with Cook's stern eyes looking right at the invisible girls in the uncanniest way, Martha understood that she had done something very, *very* naughty indeed.

They must all go right back up to bed—

she knew that now. Silent as a moth, she tapped Rachel's arm and put a finger to her lips. She pointed to the stairs. Rachel nodded, tapped Mary, signaled her to follow Martha.

Noiselessly Martha turned and tiptoed past Cook to the stairs. Cook was so close that she could have touched Martha, if she had known Martha was there. Martha could not see Cook's face except in shadow—in the darkness it seemed as though Cook was smiling, but of course that could not be so.

Mary and Rachel crowded close behind Martha. Martha had a foot on the bottom stair when suddenly a hand reached out and grabbed her. Fingers closed around her arm; Martha jumped and let out a scream that was all air and no sound.

"Hush now," said Cook softly, in a whispering voice that was choking back laughter. "Ye'll wake the house."

Martha found her breath again. It was only Cook's hand, clutching her arm. "How did you ken I was there?" she whispered. But Cook touched a finger to Martha's lips and gave her a little shove toward the kitchen. Mary and Rachel followed anxiously.

"Hush now," Cook said again. She ushered the girls to the back of the kitchen. "Mind ye dinna step on Hedgie," she warned. "This is his prowlin' time."

Martha's heart would not stop pounding. Cook sat the girls down on a bench near the fire and stoked the smoldering peat. Bustling about, with her long braid twitching like a cat's tail, she stoked the fire and put some milk in a kettle to heat. Martha and her cousins sat huddled on their bench, not daring to speak. There was a snuffling sound near the flour barrels: Hedgie, hunting for his dinner.

At last Martha asked, in a small voice, "How could you see us? We're meant to be invisible."

Cook snorted. "So ye said. Heard ye talkin', I did, as I was comin' through the kitchen to see what all the rustlin' was up front. Och, such a fright ye gave me, wakin' me up from a sound sleep as ye did! I was aye thinkin' a robber had burst into the house. Ye're that lucky I didna crown ye with me best fryin' pan."

She poured the warm milk into a cup and gave it to the girls to share. Then, pulling up a stool and sitting down squarely in front of them, she demanded to know what they had been up to. Sheepishly Martha told Cook the whole story.

Cook had almost laughed when they were in the hallway, and Martha hoped she would laugh now. But Cook's face was stern and solemn, and she shook her head from side to side. Rachel and Mary sat quiet as stones beside Martha.

"Och, Martha Gráinne Morse," Cook said, "I'd have thought ye had more sense. Draggin' your poor cousins out in the middle o' the night, and feedin' them seeds that might have poisoned the lot o' ye, for all ye kenned!"

Martha's heart gave a sickening thump. She had not thought about that. Rachel gasped in horror. "Are fern seeds poison?" she wailed.

"Nay," said Cook soothingly. "Lucky for ye. Och, when I think what might have happened to ye, wanderin' about out o' doors in the night air. Ye might have taken your death of cold, or fallen into the loch, or tripped and broken all your legs. The idea!" Her broad shoulders shuddered under the voluminous nightgown.

Martha felt like sinking into the floor. "Cook," she asked miserably, "why didna the magic work?"

"Whisht!" cried Cook. "It's glad ye should be that it didna. Messin' about with magic spells and such. It's one thing in a story, Martha, but ye ken what the minister says in kirk. Good Christian lasses like yerselves ought to ken better than to fool with enchantments and spells."

Martha remembered—now. She had not thought of it before. She had only wanted to make herself invisible.

"Mary, you're hogging all the milk," Rachel scolded. Cook clucked her tongue and got up to fill the mug again.

"Wasna it midnight?" Mary asked. "Is that why it didn't work?"

The Best-Laid Schemes

"Nivver ye mind why it didna work," Cook said, handing Martha the milk. "Ye'd have been in a terrible lot o' trouble if it had. Have ye no heard the tale about the lass who nivver was seen no more? She went out o' her father's house in the middle o' the night on Midsummer's Eve and stood beneath a waterfall with a crow's egg in her pocket, for she'd heard that was a way to make yourself invisible. Why she was fool enough to want such a thing, I canna say." Cook fixed Martha with a stern glare. Martha squirmed on the bench and pretended to be very occupied with drinking the good warm milk.

"Well, this lass, she got what she wanted, for when she came out from the waterfall, she was good and invisible, she was. Not a soul could see her for the rest o' her life. Her poor mither and father, they thought she must have fallen into a loch and drowned. They held a funeral for her, and the lass crept into the kirk and had to sit there watching her mither's heart break in two. Sure and the lass tried to speak up and tell everyone she was as alive as she'd ivver been, but that just made it worse. They all thought the voice they were hearin' belonged to a ghost, and they carried on so that the lass had to give it up and go away. She might as well have been a ghost, for no one ivver saw or spoke to her again.

"So ye see," Cook finished, "ye came off lucky, ye did."

Martha and the cousins shuddered. Yes, they agreed, it certainly was lucky for them that the magic hadn't worked after all. But Martha still wished she could have gone across the lake to see her mother.

After Kirk

Cook did not tell Father what the girls had done. For the next two days she gave Martha a lot of knowing looks with her eyebrows severely raised, but she didn't say one word about the midnight adventure. Then it was baking day, and Cook was too busy to spare time even on knowing looks.

Saturday night was to be Rachel and Mary's last night in the Stone House. At bedtime Mary cried because it would be her last time sleeping in the box bed.

"But we've such a lovely new bed in the big house," Rachel said soothingly. "I expect Mother will have the curtains hung round it by now. You should see them, Martha, they're so beautiful."

"I will see them," Martha said, pulling her nightgown over her head. "I'm going to visit you often. Mum said so. She says there'll be comings and goings between the Stone House and Fairlie all the time."

Rachel was tying the laces of Mary's nightgown in a motherly way. "I should think your family would want to come to Fairlie most of the time," she said. "It's so very much larger—remember how cramped we all were here, at Hogmanay? And Fairlie's so grand and lovely, now that my father has fixed it up some. Why didn't your father fix it up ages ago, Martha? I should think you'd rather live there than in this wee house. It hasna even a proper name."

"The Stone House is every bit as good a name as Fairlie!" Martha said hotly, yanking her hair out from under the collar of her gown.

"And it's far nicer on this side o' the loch. We've got the Creag over here on our side, and Auld Mary, and the fir wood, and everything!"

Rachel answered in a maddeningly patient voice. "Well, not *everything*. We've got the village on our side, the kirk and your brother's school and the shops and all that. And we're going to have a fir wood, too. My papa's overseer is likely setting out the saplings this minute!"

Martha felt boiling over inside. "You've not got anything—not really," she flashed. "It all belongs to my father, Fairlie and the Stone House both. *Your* father is only leasing."

She was sorry as soon as she said it. Rachel flushed red, and her mouth was a thin little line.

Mary broke in pleadingly. "Please don't fight."

"Who's fightin'?" said Mollie's brisk voice at the nursery door. She had come in to tuck the girls into bed. "Dinna tell me ye're fightin' now, on your last night together. And after ye've

187

had such a lovely visit! Now then, make it up like good lasses, and say your prayers. Ye mustna let the sun set on your anger, ye ken."

Ha, Martha thought stubbornly, *then I can be angry for a long time yet.* It was only eight o'clock; the summer sun would not set for hours. She still felt hot and churning inside. But Mollie was watching her expectantly, in a way that meant she had no doubt Martha would be a good girl and make up the quarrel. Rachel was staring miserably at the floor.

Martha sighed. "Beg pardon, Rachel," she muttered in a tight little voice.

"I-beg-your-pardon-too," Rachel said, all in a rush.

Mollie's bright voice was a bit too loud for the quiet room. "That's me good lasses. Let's hear your prayers, then, and tomorrow ye shall see your mithers!"

That was such a cheerful thought that everyone felt better. The quarrel was quite forgotten by the time Martha snuggled into the cool linen bedding between her cousins.

The next day was Sunday. That morning

everyone was in a rush to get dressed for kirk. There had not been a preaching in weeks, for the minister spent part of every summer in Lochearnhead, many miles to the south. Martha was glad he had returned, for she loved to go to the village on Sundays and see all the people of the valley assembled in the little stone kirk.

Mollie dressed Rachel and Mary in the white frocks they had been wearing when they arrived, with the smooth pale sashes tied under their arms. The dresses had not been worn all week, and so they looked just as neat and fresh as they had the first day. Only Rachel's much-chewed pink hair ribbon gave a hint as to the busy week the girls had had.

The day before, Mollie had spent half the afternoon doing a washing, and sprinkling Martha's dresses and ironing them. Now she brought out Martha's own white lawn dress and helped her to put it on—though she was fulls of doubts about the wisdom of entrusting such a snowy frock to Martha's care. She made Martha put on stockings and shoes, much to Martha's disgust.

"Please, canna I leave them off?" Martha begged. "They slow me down so."

"Good! Ye ought not to be runnin' about in that frock, anyway!" Mollie said firmly. "Ye look bright and fresh as a lily right now, and ye must stay that way at least until your mither gets a look at ye. I declare, that green ribbon does look well against your hair!"

Father met the girls in the parlor for Sunday-morning prayers. He looked splendid in his new kilt and jacket. Mollie had brushed his wig for him until it looked almost as neat as when Mum fixed it.

It was a glorious, bright, whirling summer day. Everyone was very happy on the boat ride across the lake, though it had to be a calm, quiet, Sunday kind of happiness. The ferry-man's boat was crowded; Cook and the maids squeezed on alongside Father and Martha and the cousins. There was baggage, too, for of course Rachel and Mary would go home with their parents after kirk.

Father sat close beside Martha and pointed

out a fish hawk, swooping down to snatch a fish out of the glittering water. He showed her a tall, spindly-trunked pine tree on the opposite shore, where the fish hawk had its nest.

"There've been hawks in that tree since I was a lad," he said. "I used to sneak away from me lessons and come to the loch to watch them. Think they're the royalty o' the valley, they do."

Then he fixed Martha with his stern gaze and said of course it had been very naughty of him to run away from lessons, and he trusted she was too wise ever to do such a thing. But his eyes were twinkling, and for a moment Martha wished the boat ride would go on forever. Then she thought of Mum waiting in the kirk, and she thought she couldn't wait another minute to see her.

The boat reached the far shore; the ferryman helped Martha and the cousins climb out onto the land. The tassels on Father's knee-stockings swung from side to side when he jumped off of the boat. The ferryman pushed off into the water again, to go back across the lake and pick up a last group of Glencaraid churchgoers.

Then came the walk to the village along-side the languid stream, with the feathery arbutus all around, and the spicy smell of crushed wintergreen under their feet. Martha's feet wanted to hurry to Mum; the bothersome shoes made her feel as heavy-footed as an ox. Even so, she roved far ahead of her father and the cousins, until Father called to her to wait. They all crossed the stone bridge together into Clachan and walked along the main street past the closed-up shops till they came to the small stone kirk.

When Martha entered the kirk, her eyes went right away toward her family's bench at the front. Mum was already seated there, between Grisie and Aunt Grisell. Martha's first sight of her was like catching the first scent of heather on the wind in the spring. Mum's blue silk dress seemed like an old friend.

Martha wanted to run to Mum and hug her and tell her everything that had happened dur-ing the week—even about the fern seeds; she knew she must tell Mum about the naughty parts as well as the good. But of course she could not run or hug or say anything, good or bad, in the kirk. She went quietly to the bench, as quietly as she could in her heavy shoes, and squeezed past Uncle Harry and Aunt Grisell to get next to Mum. Uncle Harry grinned at her as she went past and pinched her cheek. He looked just as he had last winter, big and bristly and jolly. Aunt Grisell, who was jiggling baby Eamonn on her lap, smiled at Martha and turned to look at Mary and Rachel, who were coming up the aisle with Father.

Mum made room for Martha to sit down beside her. She took Martha's hand in hers and squeezed it, and her blue eyes were glad and smiling. Martha leaned into Mum's side and felt the cool blue silk against her cheek. She breathed in the smell of the violet water Mum dabbed on her neck in the mornings. The same lump that had been in Martha's throat when Mum left for Fairlie was back in her throat now. But this time it was a happy lump, and Martha didn't mind its being there so much.

On the far end of the bench, Duncan leaned forward and grinned at Martha. Martha felt nearly bursting inside with gladness at seeing him again. She looked around for Grisie but did not see her at first. Then she realized with a shock that one of the three tall, silk-clad girls on the next bench was her own sister. Grisie looked so elegant and graceful that Martha hadn't recognized her just at first. Grisie gave Martha a little wave, but she was more absorbed with listening to something one of the other silk girls was whispering in her ear. Martha saw that they were Janet and Meg. She hadn't time to try to figure out which was which, for Mum nudged her with an elbow to tell her she must face front and sit properly.

Even being scolded by Mum was a lovely thing, after being away from her for so long.

It was a long and dizzying day. First the lengthy morning service, and afterward, outside the kirk, a chance at last to run into Mum's arms. But there was hardly a chance to talk to her, for there were so many grown-ups about who had such a great deal to say to each other. In a noisy mass Martha's family and Uncle Harry's family went next door to the minister's house for dinner. The children were put at a separate table in the back parlor. Grisie, Meg, and Janet sat at the main table with the grown-ups. Martha hardly noticed her food, she had so much to tell Duncan. Duncan said he liked staying at Fairlie because he did not have to get up so early in the mornings before school, but Martha could tell he had missed her.

After the meal, it was back to the kirk for the second service, and after that a long time of standing about in front while Mum and Father and Uncle and Aunt chatted with each other. Martha entertained herself by pointing out to Mary and Rachel who everyone was—the webster, the blacksmith, Duncan's schoolmaster; the webster's son Gerald, who was talking quietly to Nannie near the kirk steps; Lew Tucker and Ian Cameron.

Martha realized with a shock that although

Rachel and Mary had lived a whole week at the Stone House, they had not spent any time with Mrs. Sandy or her children, or baby Allan Tervish, or any of the Glencaraid cottagers. That was very odd, for Martha could not remember ever passing a week without stopping into any of the cottages for a visit. She had been so busy inventing games for the cousins, she had not thought about it.

Suddenly it was time to go home, and the village street rang with good-byes. Clusters of Glencaraid folk drifted off toward the lake. Cook and Nannie and Mollie had gone home already. Martha supposed they had gone ahead to have a hot supper waiting for Mum.

But to her immense surprise, Mum and Father climbed into Uncle Harry's carriage and called to the children not to dawdle on the walk back to Fairlie.

"What do they mean?" she asked Duncan, bewildered.

"Why, you're coming back to Fairlie, of course. We're all to spend the week there together. Didna you ken?"

After Kirk

"Nay!" cried Martha, watching Uncle Harry's carriage rattle out of the village and over the stone bridge. Once across, it turned off the main path onto a bumpy lane that led, Martha knew, toward Fairlie and the South Loch farm. She had often watched cottagers disappear down that lane after kirk. The main road ran directly to Loch Caraid, but the grassy South Loch lane cut at an angle across a gorse-studded moor, behind the hayfields and cow pastures of the villagers. Fairlie stood perhaps a mile outside the village, at the foot of a mountain that overlooked Loch Caraid and the valley of Glencaraid. All these things Martha knew from hearing them spoken of, but she had never set a foot upon the South Loch lane.

Grisie and the cousins were standing in the lane now, beckoning impatiently for Martha and Duncan to join them. Mary was beaming, and she jumped up and down a little as she called out to Martha how lovely it was that Martha was coming home with them.

"Now you'll see Fairlie really and truly!" she

cried, and the taller of the two young-lady cousins (Martha felt certain she was Janet) looked shocked and scolded Mary for shouting.

"Come, Martha dear, are you going to stand there all day?" Janet called solicitously. Privately, Martha didn't see the difference between Mary's shouting and Janet's calling, but she was feeling much too dazed to give it any notice. She had wanted to go to Fairlie, and now she was going. But it was so surprising, to find yourself going to another house when you had expected to go home. Stumblingly she hurried after Duncan to join the others. She could not understand why no one had told her this was the plan.

"I thought you and Mum were coming home today," she said to Grisie, in a rather accusing tone. "No one told me it would be this way round. Why didna anyone tell me?"

"I expect they thought you knew," Grisie said, looking amused. "Didna you see Sandy putting your baggage onto the raft?"

"*My* baggage? I thought it was Mary and Rachel's!"

"Some of it was, and some was yours, you goose. I saw Father put it into the carriage. I should think you'd recognize the black packing case as ours. It has Father's initials on it, after all, and not Uncle Harry's."

Martha felt silly. She had looked at that packing case and thought how much it resembled Father's. As she followed the others to Fairlie, her head was spinning with remembering things Cook and Mollie had done that ought to have told her what the plan was. She had thought Mum was coming home, but now she could not remember actually hearing anyone say so. She could see, now, that Mollie would not have spent the whole of yesterday washing and ironing Martha's clothes, if Mum had really been coming home—she'd have been busy dusting and scrubbing and polishing to make the house sparkle for Mum instead.

The long-dreamed-of walk along the South Loch path was quite spoiled for Martha, for her mind would not stop puzzling long enough for her to notice anything she passed. Her only consolation was that Mary and Rachel had been just as in the dark as she was. Martha remembered last night, when Rachel had gone on about how she couldn't wait to show Martha the new curtains hung around her bed. None of them had guessed that Martha would be seeing those curtains today!

"Martha, look," said Duncan, taking her arm. He was pointing to a spot halfway up the steep, darkening mountainside that reared ahead of them. The path was climbing gradually upward, above the floor of the valley.

"See there, on that hill? That's where Edward MacNab stood when the water fairy turned him to stone. You ken the tale."

"Nay, that canna be right!" Martha retorted. Mum had told her the story many times: how long ago one of Martha's ancestors had stood in a high place looking down on the lake, and had been so foolish as to utter a criticism of it in the hearing of the water fairy who lived there. The fairy had turned him to stone as a punishment—but only for a year, and after that they had made friends, and

After Kirk

Edward MacNab had built his house on the lakeshore.

"Edward was on the Creag when he looked down at the loch," insisted Martha. "I'm sure of it."

Duncan shook his head. "I used to think so too, when I was little. It's only because you've been up there so many times that you think it was the Creag. But the Creag's only a hill, and Mum always says Edward was on a *mountain*. If you could go up on this mountain, you'd see the same view of the valley that Edward saw. And of course when the fairy turned him back to flesh, he came down from the mountain and built his house overlooking the loch, just where Fairlie is today."

Martha opened her mouth and closed it again. The world was turned around backward. You could stand in one place and look at the world all around you, and know that you were in the very center of things, at the heart, the starting point—you could spend your whole life knowing for a certainty that this was so, and then suddenly the world wheeled around and showed you that the place you had taken for the center was really just a point out on the edge of things.

Martha felt all in a muddle. She was almost angry, and yet she didn't know why; she ought to be thrilled that she was going to see Fairlie at last. Everything was upside down.

They came around a curve, and there was Fairlie. It was a tall and imposing house, with three rows of windows staring out from its smooth stone face. There was a pointed gable above the top floor, and behind that the neat slope of the roof, with a fat chimney at either end. The wide front door was painted red. On either side of the door, the house seemed to stretch out an impossible length. Martha thought wonderingly that you could fit two Stone Houses inside.

Jutting out from one side of the big house was a smaller chunk of building, with black turf walls and a newly thatched roof; it had an open chimney like the ones Martha had seen in the cottagers' huts over on her side of the lake, with a slate covering to keep out rain. This, Martha guessed, must be the kitchen—the dark, smoky old kitchen where the mouse had fallen from the rafters into Father's soup. But it did not, from the outside at least, seem dark and smoky now. Everything looked very neat and shining in the golden light that rolled down off the mountain from the setting sun. The sun seemed to be resting a moment at the top of the mountain—Edward MacNab's mountain—before dropping into the dark night on the other side.

Martha stood very still, looking at Fairlie. It looked exactly as Mum had described, and not at all as Martha had imagined. Then Duncan called back to her, asking what was the matter, had she turned to stone? Martha jumped a little and hurried toward the house behind her brother.

Night in the Grand House

The afternoon kirk service had run very long so it was nearly suppertime when Martha and the others got to Fairlie. That night Martha did not see much more of the old house than a glimpsed view of the great hall as she was ushered through, past passages on the right and left, by a warmly smiling Mum. Mum took her hand and led her up a very wide staircase, behind the other children. Everyone else seemed to know where to go already, and then Martha remembered that she was the only one who had not seen Fairlie yet.

The stairs ended at a wide place that had more stairs at the end of it. But Rachel and Mary did not go up the new stairs; they followed Aunt Grisell down another passage and went into a room on the left. Mum and Martha went in behind them. Grisie and Janet and Meg disappeared down the passage into another room. Martha didn't know where Duncan had gone.

This room had a small fireplace and a tall cabinet and several chairs. There was a shelf with four or five books on it. Near the window was a low table, and in one corner of the room was a writing desk and a very high stool. Across the room there was an open doorway through which Martha could see a large bed hung with rose-colored curtains. Then she knew that was the nursery, where Mary and Rachel slept.

Mum said the room she was in was the nursery sitting room. Aunt Grisell helped Mary and Rachel hang their bonnets on pegs behind

the door. Then Rachel hurried into the nursery to admire the new bed-curtains. Martha
heard her cooing over the window draperies
and the striped wallpaper. It seemed a great
deal had been done to the house during the
week Mary and Rachel had been away.

The whole evening felt something like a
dream. Martha was very glad to see Mum,
and terribly curious about Fairlie. But she
could not talk to Mum and explore the house
at the same time. At any rate, there seemed
to be no question of exploring the nooks and
crannies of Fairlie this evening. Aunt Grisell
announced that supper would be sent up for
the girls shortly, and Duncan would eat with
them in the nursery.

"I must go and see to the baby," she said
to Mum in her soft voice. "We shall sup in
the spence this evening, Margaret."

She went out of the room, and Martha turned
to Mum. She didn't want Mum to leave yet.

"Canna we eat supper with you?" she
begged.

"Nay, darling, Aunt Grisell has made her

plans already." But Mum touched Martha's hair and said she would stay for a little while. The grown-ups were going to have a late supper, after the children had been put to bed.

A maid came in with a tray of bread and milk. She was a girl about Grisie's age, her small face almost lost beneath the broad ruffle of her cap. She moved very carefully, taking things off the tray and putting them on the low table by the window. Martha realized she knew the girl; she was Nannie's sister.

"Helen!" Martha cried. Helen blushed and looked as if she didn't know whether to speak or not.

Mum said lightly, "Aye, Helen's come to live on this side o' the loch now."

"I'm that glad, too; it's such a lovely house," said Helen shyly.

It all made Martha feel very strange, but she did not know why. She thought suddenly of Nannie at home in the kitchen with Cook and Mollie. They would be cleaning up the supper dishes now—but no, of course there would be no dishes to clean except their own, for the Stone House was almost empty tonight. With a pang Martha remembered that she had not said good-bye to Hedgie—she hadn't said good-bye to anyone. She had not known she would not be coming home after kirk.

She had never spent a night away from the Stone House before. It was horrible to think of the empty rooms at home, and Hedgie expecting her to appear with the little bit of bread or bacon Martha always gave him for an evening treat. She hoped Cook would remember. And who would change his water while she was gone, or bring in fresh straw for his bed?

Mum saw her stricken face. "Why, Martha, lass, whatever's the matter?"

Martha poured it all out, and Mum stroked her hair and soothed her. She said Martha wasn't to worry about a thing; Cook and the maids would see that Hedgie had everything he needed.

"Treat that animal like royalty, they do," Mum said. "Especially Cook, for all she pretends not to care two peas for him."

She folded her arms across her chest and shook her head darkly, in just the way that Cook did when she was in a grumbling frame of mind. "'Where is the wee beast?'" Mum said, in Cook's broad voice. "'Up to his snoot in trouble, most like, or lyin' in wait to run under me feet and trip me up, the wretched creature. Come oot now, Beast—and eat up this nice big dish o' the laird's best beef I've chopped into tiny wee bits for ye!'"

It was so exactly like Cook that Martha had to laugh. Rachel and Mary laughed too, for they had stayed long enough at the Stone House to know what Cook was like. Duncan came in and wanted to know what was so funny, and they kept giggling about it all through supper.

But that night, after she had been tucked into the unfamiliar bed beside Rachel and Mary with nothing but a curtain to separate her from the night, Martha thought again of home, far across the lake. She longed for her safe, cozy box bed with the door-panel that closed tight against the nighttime world. She couldn't fall asleep in this strange bed. The bed curtain billowed and swayed mysteriously, and there were noises and rustlings all around. Mary and Rachel were not a bit bothered; their deep slumbering breaths only added to the rustling.

Martha was not afraid, exactly. But she did not know this house's sounds at all. She didn't know in which room Mum and Father were sleeping, or Duncan, or Grisie. Fairlie did not seem a friendly house, like the Stone House. People were scattered about all over the place, like birds roosting on the various branches of a tree. The Stone House was like a cozy little mouse's nest.

But that thought made Martha think of the Robert Burns poem Father had read all those weeks ago, and the rest of her night was haunted by a dream of a great huge plow coming and cutting right through the walls of the Stone House, turning the whole house upside down.

Fairlie, In and Out

In the daylight, Fairlie was a little friendlier. The bashful housemaid, Helen, brought bowls of porridge for the girls' breakfast. There was a bowl for Duncan, too, and he appeared in the nursery wearing his school clothes. Martha wished he could stay home from school for one day at least. She thought of Alisdair and Robbie, far away in Edinburgh with the cousins, David and Harold. Somehow being in a strange house made her want her family all around her.

As soon as Duncan had gulped down his

porridge, he said good-bye and left for school. Martha heard Mum's voice greet him in the passage outside the nursery door, and then Mum came into the nursery. She helped Martha into her dust-gown, and she brushed Martha's hair. Having her hair brushed by Mum was one of the nicest things in the world, Martha thought, for Mum was as cheerful as Mollie and as gentle-handed as Grisie.

As she fastened a ribbon around Martha's curls, Mum told Rachel and Mary they ought to show Martha around Fairlie. But first she made Martha put on her shoes. Martha was surprised. She had never worn shoes inside the house during the summer before. This was another upside-down thing about Fairlie.

Rachel and Mary took her downstairs to the main floor. At last Martha got to see the ballroom she had heard so much about. It seemed to be just a big open room with a polished floor and a great many chairs ranged along the walls. She saw the dining room, and the music room (only there were no musical instruments in it yet), and an ornately furnished room where Mum and Father slept. Rachel called this last room the "Blue Room," which Martha thought was very funny, as there was not a bit of blue in it. Rachel explained that her mother had not liked the faded blue draperies that had hung there, and she had redecorated with curtains of a rich mustard-colored brocade.

"Why dinna you call it the Yellow Room, then?" Martha asked.

Rachel looked at her as if she had two heads. "Because it would be breaking with *tradition*, Martha. My mother says this has been called the Blue Room for two hundred years."

Martha did not see why it was all right to break tradition by changing the room's color but such a scandalous thing to change the room's name. It seemed undignified, some-how, for the Blue Room to go on wearing a name that no longer fit it. But she never could get Rachel to see her point.

There were some rooms Rachel and Mary were not permitted to enter, but they let Martha open the doors and have a look inside. There was an untidy chamber with books and papers piled on a desk; this was Uncle Harry's study. Another room was full of shiny black-painted furniture and had a loudly ticking clock on a high shelf. Rachel said this was the parlor. Martha had only a quick glimpse of this room, for Aunt Grisell came down the hall and said the little girls must not go in.

"I'm afraid it's a bit more formal than your mother's parlor, Martha dear. Little children mustn't go in unless they're invited."

Martha blinked at Aunt Grisell in surprise. She could not think of a single corner of the Stone House from which children were banned. Aunt Grisell patted her on the head and went on down the passage.

Fairlie was full of passages; Martha could not keep them all straight. Fairlie was full of people, too, or so it seemed. Every time Martha turned a corner there was another stranger to meet—there was old Albert, the steward; and his gray-haired daughter, Alice, the housekeeper; and the new understeward, a stout young man called Cappy who was the son of one of the South Loch farmers.

But to Martha's astonishment, she did not meet the cook. She did not get to so much as peek inside the black-raftered kitchen. Uncle Harry and Aunt Grisell had brought a French cook with them from Edinburgh, and Alice-the-housekeeper informed Martha that Monsieur Philippe did not take kindly to children running in and out of his kitchen.

There were so many surprises rolled up in that one piece of information that Martha hardly knew what to say. Imagine a house where you were never allowed to help in the kitchen!

Later that morning she confided her astonishment to Mary and Rachel. "I was thinking we might ask some boys I ken to find a hedgehog for your house," she said. "But what's the use, if you couldna go into the larder to play with him?"

"I dinna think Philippe would allow a hedger in his kitchen," Mary said gloomily.

Rachel added matter-of-factly, "Anyway, we don't have a beetle problem at Fairlie."

"Yet," Martha retorted. "You've only just

moved in. Wait until they find out you've got a full larder—you'll be overrun, I'll warrant."

She could not help but get cross with Rachel sometimes. Rachel talked as though Fairlie was a far nicer place to live than the Stone House.

What was far worse, Grisie did too. Grisie and Cousin Janet kept to themselves all that morning, sketching vases of flowers in the upstairs parlor (which, Martha was not a bit surprised to learn, was called "the spence"). Janet was the older cousin, sixteen years old, and she wore her hair heaped very high upon her head. The bodice of her gown was cut fashionably low. She was a tall, slender, gray-eyed girl with a very pretty nose that seemed always to be turned up about something. She was not, in Martha's opinion, a cozy kind of person.

But Grisie seemed to like her very much. They sat close together in the spence, chattering and pretending to draw. (As far as Martha could tell, they were not actually doing much drawing.)

Martha heard Grisie tell Janet that she wished she could always live at Fairlie. "I canna understand why Father ever gave up living at Fairlie in the first place," Grisie said. "He could have done the same things to fix it up that Uncle Harry has done."

"Och, well," said Janet delicately, "my mother says your father cares more about his fir wood than he does about the roof over his head."

It made Martha boiling mad to hear Janet and Grisie talk like that. "So what if he does?" she demanded. "It'll be the finest wood in the county, when it's full grown! Our side o' the loch is the best land in all of Scotland!"

"Hush, Martha," Grisie scolded. "Dinna interrupt. No one was speaking to you."

Martha stared at her sister, outraged. She turned on her heel and stalked out of the room. Sometimes it seemed as though a stranger had come and taken the place of her sister. Martha wanted to go and find Mum, but she hardly knew where to begin looking in this big, rambling house.

Mary and Rachel caught up to her in the great hall. Martha felt embarrassed to see them. They had heard Grisie rebuke her. It was hardly to be borne, being scolded by your own sister in front of your cousins. Martha felt suddenly that she was sick of cousins, and sisters too for that matter. She wished she could go home.

"You havena seen Meg and Janet's room yet," Rachel said to Martha.

"It doesna matter," Martha said. She did not much want to see anything having to do with cousin Janet.

But Mary said, "Come, you must see the peacock rug!" And in spite of herself, Martha felt a glimmer of interest—a peacock rug! What on earth could that be?

Cousin Meg was in her room, sitting at a low table by the window, writing something in a cloth-covered book. She looked up and smiled when the girls came in.

"Hullo, Martha," Meg said. "I scarcely had a chance to see you yesterday."

To Martha's surprise Meg was quite nice to

be with. She invited the girls in and took a book called *Tom Thumb's Nursery Rhymes* off the shelf for them to look at. But at first Martha could not look at anything but the peacock rug. It was one of the most wonderful things she had ever seen. It was like a great thick woolen blanket spread upon the floor in the center of the room, springy beneath her shoes. A pattern was woven into the wool—a wide border of giant, flat, tuliplike flowers with a beautiful blue-and-green bird in the center. The bird's tail was spread open like a fan. It had a long slender neck and a yellow beak.

Rachel and Mary sat upon the rug and turned the pages of Meg's book. Martha lay down with her face close to the rug and stared at that peacock. Up close she could see that he was nothing but little loops of colored wool pulled through a canvas mesh, but when she stood up he was a proud and glorious bird again.

"It's lovely, isna it?" Meg asked. "Papa bought it last winter, in town."

Cousin Meg was not a bit like cousin Janet, and Martha wondered how she had ever gotten them confused. Meg was fourteen years old, plump and cheerful, with large hazel eyes smiling out beneath masses of auburn hair. She was glad her family had left the Edinburgh town house. The family upstairs, she explained to Martha, had had eleven children all squeezed into two rooms. They couldn't help but make a lot of noise, Meg said, especially at night.

"There were two or three babies, as near as I could tell," she said. "It always seemed like a new baby came along before the last one had quite learned to crawl. I expect it wasn't really as quick as that, but not far from it. The poor mother couldna ever get them all quiet at once. I used to wish I could go up and help her, but of course that wouldna do."

"Why wouldna it?" Martha wanted to know, and Meg laughed and said, "Och, you are the funny one, aren't you!"

But she didn't say it in a turned-up-nose kind of way, nor in a smugly smiling way as Grisie might have done. Meg was warm and merry, and she reminded Martha a great deal of Mum.

She told Meg so, and Meg said, "I expect that's because I'm named after her. I'm really Margaret, you know. Just as your sister, Grisie, is named after my mother."

"Oh!" This was something Martha had never known before. "But," she said musingly, "Grisie's not a bit like Aunt Grisell." Aunt Grisell had a soft, kind way of speaking. Martha had never heard her snap at anybody.

But Meg said, "Och, I don't know. Grisie's pretty like Mother, and gentle, and graceful, and so awfully clever at needlework."

Martha stared wonderingly at Meg. Grisie *was* all of those things. She was all of those things so thoroughly that Martha had ceased to notice them. These days she only noticed the young-lady airs and the sharp temper—it was hard to notice anything else.

It was a strange thing, Martha thought, that there could be so many sides to people. People, it seemed to her, were very much like houses. Some houses were friendly and cozy, and you could know everything about them in a very short time. Other houses were more secretive, full of dim passages and closed doors and rooms you weren't allowed into. Sometimes you got a glimpse inside one of the rooms and saw a side of the house utterly unlike anything you would have expected to find within its walls.

By the time she had lived a few days at Fairlie, Martha had found out everything there was to know about the rooms she was allowed to go into. But there were still many rooms she knew nothing about. Fairlie was a house in which children were expected to play quietly in the nursery and not go poking around in kitchens and cupboards and other people's bedchambers.

The funny thing was, Uncle Harry kept a lot of dogs, lean-bodied hounds with serious brown eyes, and a couple of yipping terriers, and these were allowed nearly free rein in the house. They poked around wherever they pleased and did all sorts of things that even naughty children would never have dared to do. They jumped on the parlor furniture with muddy paws, and they scratched at closed doors, whining, until someone came and let them into the room.

Aunt Grisell watched them with worried eyes, but whenever she scolded one of the dogs, it would come and lay its head at her feet, looking up contritely. Then Aunt Grisell would sigh, and shake her head a little, and say, "Och, you wretched, wretched creature," in a laughing voice.

Uncle Harry never scolded the dogs at all. He laughed too and took their heads between his hands, and wrestled with them a little or scratched behind their ears. The dogs followed him all over the house, scrambling to walk beside him. The only person they loved more than Uncle Harry was the baby, little Eamonn, who was walking now, toddling on unsteady feet in his newly shortened skirts. Sometimes he walked between two of the dogs, clutching handfuls of fur on either side. The dogs were always gentle with Eamonn, and they never jumped or jostled when he was on the floor.

At mealtimes they lay under the table near Uncle Harry's chair. He fed them tidbits from his plate. Mum teased that Uncle might as well have chairs brought to the table for the dogs to sit upon, he spoiled them so.

Much of the time, Uncle Harry and the dogs and Father were out of the house, hunting. They went far beyond the fields of South Loch to lonely places where pheasants nested in the tall grass.

Then the house was very quiet, and all the doors were shut again.

Martha longed to go with Father and Uncle and the lolloping, noisy dogs. When they were gone, Fairlie was so hushed and calm, she wanted to shout.

Aunt Grisell did not like her girls to play outside; she said it was hard enough keeping a clean house when you had dogs running in and out. But one afternoon when little Eamonn was having trouble settling down for his nap, she suggested in a bright voice that perhaps Martha should go out for a bit of a walk.

Martha leaped up at once. She took off

her shoes and stockings and ran to the nursery to put them away. Janet asked her if she didn't have things rather the wrong way around, taking her shoes *off* to go outside.

"It's no as though today's a Sunday," Martha retorted. Her toes wiggled their happiness over being free.

Mary wanted to go too, but Aunt Grisell said she must keep her shoes on.

The world outside Fairlie was warm and bright. Martha's heart was soaring, just from the feeling of wind in her hair and sun on her face.

"Let's climb Edward MacNab's mountain," she told Mary.

They could not climb all the way to the top, of course. But they went around behind Fairlie and walked a long way up the slope. The ground was scrubby and uneven, with clumps of bushes here and there, and a thick carpet of heather. The heather's purple bell-shaped flowers held out their sweet perfume for the wind to carry. Heather smelled just as lovely on this side of the lake as it did at the Stone House.

Mary didn't know anything at all about outside. She could not tell a bilberry bush from a gorse bush, nor a corbie from a crow. Martha had fun telling her the names of things.

She showed Mary a mushroom ring in the grass.

"You must be careful never to set foot inside it," Martha warned, "or the fairies will put you to sleep and you'll not wake up for a hundred years. Your mother and father and all the rest of us would be long dead, and it'd be our grandchildren you'd find living in our houses."

Mary's eyes were very wide. She begged Martha to tell her more stories like that. So they sat down on the heather and watched the bees fill their saddlebags with nectar, while Martha told Mary all about Edward MacNab, and the water fairy who had turned him to stone.

"Duncan says it happened right here," Martha said. "Edward would have had the selfsame view o' the valley as we do now. Except the house wouldna be there, nor the barns and the fir plantation."

The Fairlie grounds were sprawled out beneath them. They could not see much of the South Loch farm from where they sat— only the long neat rows of baby trees that had been tucked carefully into the ground on the slope behind the house and barns. The cottagers' huts were out of sight around the curve of the mountain. But Martha could see clear across the lake from here, all the way to a pointed gray hill jutting into the sky far opposite, that she thought must be the Creag. She couldn't see the Stone House, for the curve of the mountain cut off the view of the lake's northern side.

She felt prickly inside, looking at her lake and her own favorite hill from this strange vantage point. The Creag was where she had always gone to have a look at the world all around. To think that all the time anyone sitting here on this mountain could have been staring right at her! Only perhaps she would have been too small to be seen. It made her feel invisible, and she didn't like the feeling.

She was glad that the trick with the fern seeds had not worked, after all.

"I wonder," she said, to hear her voice out loud. She didn't know what she wondered. Mary was looking at her quizzically, so Martha said, "I wonder what they're doing at home."

"The same things they were doing when we left, I expect," said Mary. "Eamonn is sleeping, and Rachel is sewing, and—"

"Nay," Martha broke in. "I meant at my home. The Stone House."

But she supposed Mary was right. Over there across the lake, Cook and Nannie and Mollie and Sandy would all be going about their work, just as they did when the family was there. They wouldn't know that Martha was thinking about them right at that moment, and missing them.

The Terrier's Song

Because Fairlie was so close to the village, visitors came calling more often than they did at the Stone House. Martha could not remember ever seeing so many guests in one week as she saw during that week at Fairlie. The lady and gentleman who leased Father's Glenmorris farm came to pay their respects, and the minister came for dinner one day. Other people dropped in for cups of tea or ale, to talk politely about the weather while stealing glances at the wallpaper and the sideboard. Mum said all the county was curious to see what Uncle had done to the house.

The kindly old laird of Alroch came to visit, but that was not a surprise; he lived just on the other side of the mountain and he was Mum and Father's good friend. He had spent many a night in the spare bed in the Stone House parlor. At Fairlie there was a whole extra room just to put overnight guests in. Mr. Alroch said it warmed his heart to see the old house looking just as grand as it had when he was a young man and Father's parents were newly wed. But after dinner the first day, he whispered to Martha that he'd trade all the rich dishes concocted by Uncle Harry's fancy cook for a plate of Cook's good Stone House bannocks any day.

Martha agreed with him wholeheartedly. She did not like her meat smothered with sauce the way Monsieur Philippe served it. And she hated the slippery feel of *mousse* on her tongue. That was a strange kind of dish Philippe served nearly every day, a squishy sort of pudding made of finely chopped fish.

Mr. Alroch did not stay long, only one night. But the morning after he left, more visitors came bumping toward Fairlie in a black buggy drawn by two horses.

The carriage looked very fine rolling down the avenue of lime trees, with the green leaves rustling like flags to welcome it. When it came close to the house, Martha could see that the buggy had splatters of mud on its sides, and it jolted up and down as it came forward. The horses looked tired and discouraged. A large gentleman with a frothy lace cravat and a pursed-up mouth sat holding the reins, and next to him was a lady with a lot of white hair dressed very high.

Their names were Mr. and Mrs. Biggins. Father and Mum seemed to know them well, but Martha had never seen them before. They had an estate seven or eight miles away on the other side of the village.

Mr. Biggins had on tight knee breeches and thin white stockings. His wife wore a wine-colored silk gown cut low at the bosom and sashed high above her waist. Delicate high-heeled slippers peeked out beneath the shimmering folds of her dress.

The Bigginses stayed for dinner. They had heard about Uncle Harry's French cook and were eager to know if his talents exceeded their own cook's. Each time a new dish was brought to the table, Mr. Biggins leaned forward and scrutinized it. His pursed-up mouth would twitch and he would make remarks in a muttering voice that was nevertheless audible all the way down at the children's end of the table, such as: "Eggs, eh? How very odd— rather common, I'd have thought."

Or: "This bird is rather tough, I must say."

When Mr. Biggins tasted his fish, he said it was nothing like the Loch Tay perch; he said it had been a marvelous year for perch in Loch Tay. But Martha noticed he ate three helpings of Loch Caraid perch anyway.

Mrs. Biggins ate scarcely anything. She talked instead, asking Mum and Aunt Grisell a great many questions about Edinburgh society and not stopping to wait for the answers. Martha found it maddening, because they were very interesting questions and she would have liked to hear the answers. There were a few questions she'd have liked to ask herself, but children must be seen and not heard at the table, when guests were present.

When dinner was over, they all trooped into the parlor, followed by Uncle Harry's dogs, and Mrs. Biggins sang for everyone. She stood with her hands folded on her chest and her elbows held stiffly out. Her head tilted back as if weighed down by the sculpted tower of her hair. There was a small pink ribbon perched on the top of her head, like a butterfly that had stopped for a rest. When she sang the long tremulous high notes, the butterfly wings quivered.

Mrs. Biggins sang a lot of high notes. Uncle Harry's dogs lay in a shaggy heap near the door and watched her intently. Their bodies were sprawled out, but their heads kept lifting off the floor to look at Mrs. Biggins. Her high notes really were very high, and once or twice one of the dogs put up its head and made a little howling noise.

Whenever that happened, Mrs. Biggins's

eyes swiveled round to glare at the dogs. The tilt of her head never changed; only the glaring eyes moved. The rest of the time her eyes were closed, with her eyebrows arching high and bunching up the skin of her forehead in rows of wrinkles.

Uncle Harry was quick to scold the dogs. But he did not put them out, and they kept joining in with Mrs. Biggins on the highest notes. She sang for quite a long time. Martha felt fidgety in her chair, but Mum looked at her in a way that meant *Be still*.

> *"Oh, my love's like a red, red rose*
> *That's newly sprung in June;*
> *Oh, my love's like the melody*
> *That's sweetly played in tune,"*

sang Mrs. Biggins.

> *"Ow-oooo,"*

sang Uncle Harry's terrier.

Then Mrs. Biggins's song was finished, and

she bowed her head while Father and Mum and Aunt Grisell clapped. Uncle Harry ruffled the fur around the terrier's ears and told it it ought to be ashamed of itself. But later, after the Bigginses had gone away, Martha heard Uncle Harry tell Mum that he'd felt a bit like howling himself.

"Julia Biggins was ever being asked to sing at parties in town," he said, "but it takes a more patient ear than mine to appreciate her."

After that it became a joke among the children to howl whenever one of them said something the others didn't want to hear. Janet got howled at the most, because she liked to scold so much. Martha could howl the loudest, but it was Grisie, to everyone's surprise, who sounded most like a real dog. When she howled, all of Uncle Harry's dogs came running with their claws scrabbling against the floorboards, to see what strange new hound had wandered into their house.

Martha liked to hear her do it. The howling was the first thing she had liked about her sister in a very long time.

Wheep, Whaup

On Friday, Mum said it was time the Morses got home. Martha could hardly believe it had been less than a week since she had left the Stone House. Home seemed a long time ago and a great distance away.

Leaving Fairlie felt like the beginning of a long journey. The cousins said good-bye as though they were not going to see each other for a long time. Mary sobbed so hard to see Martha go that Martha felt a little tight in the throat herself. But when Rachel began to sniffle, Martha had to laugh. She doubted Rachel would really miss her that much.

Janet and Grisie clung to each other. Janet was wailing; she begged Grisie to write her the minute she touched shore. Mum laughed at them and said they were being ridiculous.

"You ken right well that you'll see one another in kirk, two days hence. Such carryings-on over nothing!"

But Grisie's eyes were tragic. Martha could see that she was crying over more than leaving Janet—Grisie did not want to leave Fairlie. Martha remembered how Grisie had told Janet she wished she could live at Fairlie all the time. Watching her sister carry on, Martha felt again that terrible feeling of wanting to shake Grisie or slap her. It was just like Grisie to spoil what ought to have been the happiest moment of the week, the going home. Martha pushed the ugly feeling down. She *would* be happy, she *would*. She could not wait to get home.

Father clapped Uncle Harry on the back and thanked him for his hospitality. He helped

Mum down the steep bank to where the ferryman's boat was waiting. Martha scrambled in beside Mum, and Grisie came behind her, still dabbing at her eyes. Duncan had gone to school as usual and would not be home until after supper that night.

But he would come home, thought Martha, and that was the main thing.

She was amazed, when the boat pulled away from the bank below Fairlie and came around the curve of the shoreline, at how quickly she could make out the cluster of cottages on the old familiar shore. A few moments later she saw her own house shining on the hill.

She half expected Cook and Nannie and Mollie to be waiting on the bank, waving their aprons at her. But there were no Glencaraid folk at all to be seen on the shore or outside the cottages, except for a single girl spreading some damp linen on the grass to bleach in the sun. It was Annie Davis, Sandy's daughter.

Annie saw the boat coming and straightened up, calling out a cheerful hallo. The cloth flapped one of its corners, and Annie bent

back to pin it beneath a stone.

"It's washday," Martha said to Mum. "Where's everyone else with the wash?"

"Mowing the hay," Mum replied. "Or pulling flax. Summer has grown tall while we've taken our leisure."

A pang went through Martha. She felt as though she'd been gone a very long time. She thought of Hedgie—suppose he had run away, because she had gone off and left him?

The instant the boat nosed the shore, Martha sprang out and ran up the path.

"Martha!" came Mum's voice behind her, but Martha was already halfway up the hill. Smoke wafted lazily out of the chimney on the kitchen side of the Stone House. The house looked small and plain after Fairlie, and cozy and snug and perfect. Martha's heart felt squeezed inside her, she was so glad to be home.

The front door stood wide open, as it always did in fine weather. The purple bells of heather blanketing Mum's bench quivered gaily in the wind. As Martha passed through the yard, she jumped onto the loupin'-on stone and leaped off again. She burst into the house, crying, "We've come home! We've come home!"

Mollie came to the top of the stairs, a dusting cloth in her hand, and called down, "Good day, Miss Martha, dear." Martha shouted a greeting to her and ran into the kitchen. There was Cook, standing at the hearth before a steaming kettle with a spoon near her lips, blowing on a taste of broth to cool it.

"Cook, we've come home!"

"So I hear," said Cook wryly, and she tasted her broth.

She nodded her head in satisfaction and turned toward Martha, setting the spoon down on the long table.

"And how was your week in the great house, then?" she asked in a pleasant, everyday manner, as if Martha went off on long visits all the time. Then she huffed in surprise, for Martha came barreling at her and threw her arms around Cook's waist.

"There, there, lass," Cook said awkwardly.

"Eh, it's glad I am to see ye as well."

Martha hardly knew what to do first, now that she was home. She found Hedgie, a slumbering lump in his nest of straw, and woke him up and nuzzled him and fed him a bit of bacon that Cook obligingly gave her. Nannie came in from the garden, a heap of plums in her apron, and greeted Martha warmly. She was eager to hear all about Fairlie, whether it was as fine as folk were saying, and how her sister Helen was getting on, and whether Martha had seen much of . . . of the village folk. Nannie blushed rosy red over the last question, and Martha could not figure out what was wrong with her until Cook snorted and said, "Did ye see young Gerald the webster's son, is what she means."

Martha understood suddenly and felt bowled over with astonishment. "Nannie," she yelped, "you have a sweetheart!

"Hush, now," Nannie murmured, blushing harder. "Dinna make a fuss over it. It'll be years yet before we can marry. Gerry wants to earn enough to set up his own shop, first."

Martha hardly had time to take in this news before Mum and Father and Grisie came into the house. Cook and Nannie went to welcome them home. Cook said she'd made a nice dinner that was ready for the table just as soon as ever the family was ready to eat.

"That sounds lovely, Cook. We'll just go upstairs and have a wash, first," said Mum.

Grisie went into the parlor and sat down at the pianoforte, and her hands flying over the keys played a lilting song that filled up the house. She looked actually happy to be home. She bent her head down and kissed the pianoforte.

"I missed you, you old thing," she said.

Martha crept up next to her. Her whole self was filled up, suddenly, with a feeling she couldn't explain. Nannie was going to get married—not soon, but someday, and probably she would leave Glencaraid when that happened. Grisie had moped all spring because Father would not let her go to school in Edinburgh, and she had said right out that she'd rather live at stuffy old Fairlie than in the Stone

House. Martha stood staring at her sister, at her serious eyes and the shining knot of her hair. She was swept again with that feeling she'd had at Fairlie that she was looking at a stranger instead of the sister she had slept next to almost every night of her life.

"Martha, what do you want?" Grisie said sharply, breaking off in the middle of her song.

"Nothing," Martha said.

"Then stop staring at me like that."

"Grisie," said Martha suddenly, "will you brush my hair tomorrow?"

Grisie had resumed playing, and she twitched her shoulders impatiently without stopping her song. "Of course I will, Martha. I always do," she said. She played on for a moment, and then, just as Martha was going to leave, Grisie's hands halted on the keys.

Grisie looked at Martha, and her eyes were kind. She reached up a hand and smoothed a lock of hair away from Martha's brow.

"Of course I will, Martha," she repeated, but all the impatience was gone from her voice. "Just like I always do."

She smiled at Martha, and Martha smiled back. Mum's voice came down the stairs, calling them to dinner.

"We'd better go up," said Grisie. She caught Martha's hand as they headed to the table.

No dinner had ever tasted as good as the plain mutton and potatoes that Mollie set before them, at the old wooden table in Mum and Father's room. Looking around the table, Martha felt a little thrill of things going back into their right places. Father sat in his chair, and Mum sat in hers, with the blue lake shining out the window beyond her. Grisie and Martha reached for the last jam-cake at the same time. Martha let her sister have it, because it was so funny to hear Grisie going on about how good the blackberry jam was that was spread between the layers of cake. Grisie didn't know that Martha had helped to make the jam.

The day felt like a holiday to Martha, and it was strange, after dinner, to see everyone scattering to do quite ordinary things. Father went out to look at the oats. Grisie sat back down at the piano and played finger exercises over and over in a numbing repetition.

Mum changed into an old linen frock and tucked her hair beneath a linen cap.

"There," she said. "I've done being a fine lady for a while. This afternoon I shall just be plain Missus Morse. Martha, whatever are your dolls doing in my spice cupboard?"

All the rest of that day, Mum was busy. But in the evening, after Duncan was home from school and supper was eaten and cleared away, she sat down by the open window of her bedroom and drew her spinning wheel near. Then only her hands were busy. The spinning wheel hummed cozily, like a cat purring. Grisie sat at her wheel, too, and the sound of her spinning was like another cat.

Father stretched his legs out before him in his big armchair, but he did not open a newspaper. Duncan set up his paints by the other window, where the light was best. With his tin soldiers arrayed in grim ranks on the windowsill, he set to work painting a battle scene of such heroic proportions that not since the

Battle of Culloden in 1745 had Scotland seen its like. Mum sang a fighting song to help him along.

"Wi' a hundred pipers and all, and all,
Wi' a hundred pipers and all, and all;
We'll up and gie them a blaw, a blaw,
Wi' a hundred pipers and all, and all.

"Oh! It's over the border awa', awa',
It's over the border awa', awa,'
We'll on and we'll march to Carlisle hall,
Wi' its gates, its castle, and all, and all."

It was all so cozy that Martha half expected Alisdair and Robbie to burst in at any moment. But of course they were still in Edinburgh, sitting exams before the holidays. Martha felt caught up in a tangle of gladness and longing. It did not seem right, somehow, that Alisdair and Robbie should be so far away when the rest of the family was happy together.

"I've missed hearing you sing these past weeks, Margaret," said Father.

"What, when you've had Julia Biggins to listen to?"

Father shuddered. "I'd sooner listen to Harry's dogs than hear that woman wail."

Mum laughed, and she sang some more.

"Whistle, whistle, auld wife,
And ye shall get a hen.
—I wadna whistle, quoth the wife,
Though ye should give me ten.

"Whistle, whistle, auld wife,
And ye shall get a cock.
—I wadna whistle, quoth the wife,
Though ye should give me a flock.

"Whistle, whistle, auld wife,
And ye shall get a gown.
—I wadna whistle, quoth the wife,
For the finest in the town.

"Whistle, whistle, auld wife,
And ye shall get a man.
—Wheep, whaup, quoth the wife,
I'll whistle if I can!"

When it came to the whistling part, Mum scrunched up her face and pursed her lips so comically that all the rest of them burst out laughing. Mum went on wheeping and whauping. Martha and Duncan tried to whistle but it was impossible to pucker when they were laughing so hard.

Grisie managed it; she let out a shrill, piercing whistle that soared above the laughter. Mum applauded, and Father raised his glass as if toasting her.

"I'll bet Grisie's been practicing," said Duncan, with a wicked grin that made him look exactly like Robbie.

Martha saw what he meant and put in saucily, "Aye, to be ready for catching herself a husband."

"What!" Grisie sputtered indignantly. "I would never—"

Then she broke off and met the teasing look in Martha's eye. A gleam came into Grisie's own eyes.

"I'd never whistle to catch a husband," she said mildly. "I'd do this!"

And then she threw back her head and howled, just as she had done at Fairlie.

"Oww-ooooo!"

Father burst out roaring. All of them were laughing, Martha and Duncan and Mum and Grisie. The whole room was filled with their laughter, bouncing and echoing off the walls, until it seemed the Stone House itself was laughing too.